FOUR YEAR VOWS

"The Exit"

J.P.Ellison

Dedicating to "To those who know love isn't perfect, but still choose it every day."

Introduction

Some stories begin with a spark. Others begin in silence — in the hollow space left behind after everything has fallen apart.

Vanessa's story begins there. In the quiet after the noise, after the courtroom lights fade, after the last door closes on a life she thought she understood. The world has not been gentle with her. It has taken things she never thought she could live without, tested the limits of her endurance, and left her to rebuild from the remnants. But even in the smallest, most fractured corners of her heart, something endures. A small, stubborn light.

Ethan knows that light well. His own story has been shaped by loss and the slow work of forgiveness — the kind that doesn't come easily, the kind that takes years to even begin. Yet when he meets Vanessa, something within him begins to settle. Their connection is quiet at first, like a breath drawn between two people who have already lived too many lifetimes of pain. It isn't about rescue. It isn't about perfection. It's about recognition — the moment two souls see each other and understand.

What grows between them is fragile but real. They learn to navigate the awkwardness of hope, to laugh again, to trust in small ways. They build something steady out of patience, apology, and grace. And from that fragile beginning, a family takes shape — not the kind that fits a perfect picture, but one born from truth, from trying, from love that keeps showing up even when it hurts.

When their daughter, Lila Grace, arrives, she becomes more than a child. She is a promise — the living embodiment of everything they fought to keep alive inside themselves. Her cry is the sound of renewal, of something unbroken pushing its way into the world. In her tiny heartbeat is the echo of every choice they made to keep going, to keep believing that love could still find them.

This story is not just about birth, or love, or the quiet miracle of a new beginning. It's about what it takes to reach that moment — the grief, the fear, the days when faith feels too far away. It's about how love can be both soft and fierce, how it can heal and still remember the pain that came before.

Vanessa and Ethan's journey is not a fairy tale. It's not about happy endings, but honest ones. It's about what it means to rebuild after loss, to choose hope when it would be easier to close your heart. It's about the kind of love that isn't loud or perfect, but lasting — the kind that keeps its promise even when the world forgets.

And in that small hospital room, where lavender and antiseptic fill the air, where a woman breathes through pain and a man whispers words that hold her steady, everything begins again.

And so, on a quiet night that smelled faintly of lavender and something sharp and clean, the past finally loosened its grip. The world outside slowed to a hush, as if it, too, was waiting. Inside a dimly lit hospital room, beneath the soft hum of machines and the whisper of nurses' shoes on polished floors, two people held on to each other and prepared to meet the rest of their lives.

It was the beginning — not of perfection, but of something true.

Table Of Contents

CHAPTER 1

The Tired Kind of Silence

The calendar had turned. Four years and two weeks had slipped quietly into history. The renewal papers were signed and tucked into the top drawer of the vanity, their edges already curling, the ink sinking into the paper like a secret the house itself was keeping.

Vanessa glanced at them, then rolled her eyes.

"Look at us," she muttered. "Still pretending we're in a Hallmark movie."

The papers didn't answer. Typical.

They had made it through another contract—another round of vows, another promise to stay. On paper, it looked like permanence. In truth, between

1

Vanessa and August, distance had crept back—slow and relentless, like water seeping through drywall. Not loud. Not stormy. Just… exhausting.

She let out an exaggerated yawn and looked up at the ceiling, as if daring it to judge her lack of enthusiasm.

Vanessa sat on the edge of the tub, lotion slick on her palms. The cap lay open beside her, the faint scent of cocoa butter softening the air. She rubbed her heels in slow, patient circles—not just easing the soreness from standing all day, but almost as if she could knead away the fatigue lodged deeper than her bones.

"Honestly," she muttered to the tub, "why don't these lotions come with a massage function?"

The bathroom light hummed above her, dim and forgiving, softened by a bulb she hadn't bothered to replace. It threw her reflection into a hazy amber glow.

In the mirror, a woman looked back—older than thirty-nine, shadows etched deep beneath her eyes, skin tired, hair twisted into a careless knot that had surrendered halfway through the day.

"Nice knot," Vanessa whispered to her reflection.

"Very avant-garde."

The woman didn't laugh.

Her reflection blinked—eyes bruised by sleepless nights, mouth pressed into a thin, uncertain line, jaw tense as if even her face had learned to brace for impact. She wasn't the woman who once believed in second chances, in renewal, in the kind of love that could be repaired.

This version of Vanessa was different. She was holding herself together not with hope, but with habit.

She sighed and muttered, "Well, habit's better than crying into cereal."

The creak of the bathroom door broke her reverie.

August filled the doorway—shoulders squared, shirtless, arms crossed against his chest. He leaned there for a moment, debating whether to enter, his figure cutting through the faint spill of light from the hallway.

Vanessa made a small noise, half laugh, half groan.

"Great," she muttered. "Here comes Mr. 'I can read your thoughts.'"

"You're still up," he said.

3

Her eyes met his in the mirror. "Couldn't sleep. Been on my feet all day." She flexed her toes dramatically and gave a faint grin. "Also, clearly winning at lotion application."

He lingered in the doorway, as though testing the air between them. Then he stepped inside, closing the distance until he leaned against the sink. His presence pressed into the room—quiet, solid, heavy. Vanessa tapped the edge of the tub, the sound sharp against the tile, as if to remind herself there was still rhythm somewhere.

"I picked up Miles from Nevaeh's," he said after a moment. "He barely spoke. Just stared out the window the whole ride."

Vanessa's chest tightened. She rubbed her ankle harder, eyes fixed on her reflection. "He's adjusting. Again. New school, new version of us. He's six, August. How many versions has he had to learn already?"

August's jaw flexed. The silence between them thinned.

"I told him we'd go to the aquarium Saturday," he

4

said quietly. "Thought it might help."

She turned her head, her face half lost in shadow. "You planned that without asking me?"

"I wanted to give him something to look forward to."

Her voice softened, though a trace of steel remained. "That's sweet," she said. "But I wanted Saturday. Not just for me—okay, yes, also for my sanity."

"I didn't take anything from you."

"I didn't say you did," she answered, smirking despite herself. "But points for trying."

He shifted closer, the scent of soap still clinging to him. "I'm trying to be a good stepdad."

The words hung there—simple, earnest, almost too fragile for the space they occupied.

The word cracked like glass. Vanessa snorted quietly under her breath. "Stepdad. Really? Can't we just call it 'adult in the room'?"

She straightened, her reflection rising behind her like a ghost witness to the rift. "I see your effort. I do. But I can't keep propping up the roof alone." Her eyes rolled upward. "I might collapse into glitter or something dramatic if this continues."

His arms folded tighter. "You think I'm not carrying anything?"

"Tell me what you carry," she said, her tone sharp but tired. "From here, it looks like bills and exhaustion. Bonus points for guilt and awkward charm."

He stepped closer, his voice splintering. "I carry the shame. Every whisper about Antigua. About Anthone. About Miles. Every smile that boy gives me feels like guilt."

Vanessa's throat closed. "Shame. Great, we can start a club." She tapped the counter lightly. "Membership includes sleepless nights and staring at lotion bottles."

The words split her open. Antigua. The test results. The papers she had signed anyway. He had never said it this raw before. She drew in a shaky breath and muttered, "Well, that escalated."

Anger surged up, burning behind her eyes. "Don't act like you're the only one bleeding," she said, voice trembling. "I didn't go to Antigua to punish you. I went because I was already disappearing."

He flinched. "And yet you signed those papers."

"I signed them because I believed we could rebuild. Because you said you'd fight for renewable love. But fighting means more than aquarium trips. It means showing up. Every day. Without points. Without credit."

His chest rose ragged, breath uneven. "Maybe I don't know how to be the man you need anymore."

Her fingers gripped the edge of the sink until her knuckles blanched. "How many more years do I wait for you to learn? Four? Eight? Another renewal?"

The silence vibrated through the room. Then August turned and walked out, his shadow sliding past the doorway.

Vanessa pressed her palms harder into the sink. "Well, at least the house isn't judging me alone."

Later, when she slipped into their bed, his side was still warm. She turned toward the wall and let the dark stare back until dawn crept in like judgment.

And through it all, one question gnawed sharper than hunger: had she signed for love, or only for habit?

She muttered softly, "Probably habit. But the good kind." Then she rolled onto her back and snorted. "Great, Vanessa. Stay married because you fold laundry like a champ."

The ceiling fan ticked in smug rhythm. Somewhere in the house, August's footsteps faded, and the silence wrapped itself tighter than Spanx.

By morning, she figured silence might actually file the divorce papers before she did.

CHAPTER 2

Paper Walls

By the time the sun came up, the joke wasn't funny anymore. The night had ended without apology.

Vanessa woke in a bed that felt wider than the ocean. August hadn't come back upstairs; his side of the sheets stayed cold, flat as paper.

By morning, silence had hardened into armor. He moved through the kitchen like a ghost—pouring coffee, avoiding her eyes. Miles filled the air with chatter about turtles and cereal, stitching sound into the empty spaces his parents refused to cross. Every word from her son scraped against her guilt.

When the knock came, it wasn't unexpected. The

process server's hand was steady as he slid the envelope across the threshold. *Petition for Dissolution under the FAR Renewal Clause.*

Vanessa signed with fingers that felt like glass. August stood behind her, arms crossed, the same way he had leaned in the bathroom doorway. His voice was flat, but it cut clean through.

"So that's it. You're really going through with it."

She didn't answer. Not because she lacked words, but because every word she had would either ignite him or break her.

That night, she sat at the vanity. The renewal papers still hid in the drawer below, ghosts pressed against her ribs. On top sat another stack—divorce filings, custody schedules, futures reduced to ink and signatures.

When the court date arrived, she wore black. Not for mourning—she refused to grant August that victory—but because armor should look like something.

She slipped on her heels, kissed Miles' forehead as he slept, and whispered the lie every survivor breathes.

"You are strong enough."

Then she walked into the courthouse.

The air inside was too clean, too cold, like it had been scrubbed of emotion. The walls hummed with the quiet shuffle of strangers—lawyers, clerks, people ending stories that once began with promise. Vanessa stood among them, steady on trembling legs, her hands folded around a purse that suddenly felt heavier than her entire past.

She thought about the vows, the papers, the small laughs they'd once shared over burnt pancakes and broken promises. Every memory seemed to echo through the marble floors, soft but unrelenting.

When her name was called, she straightened. The sound of her heels on the tile reminded her that moving forward still counted as motion, even if it hurt.

The courthouse smelled of paper and polish, lives filed away in neat folders. Vanessa sat at the petitioner's table, fingers laced so tightly her knuckles looked carved from bone. It wasn't supposed to feel like a trial, but everything about the room carried trial weight: the raised bench, the paneled walls, the silence that threatened to preserve every word forever.

Across the aisle, August slouched in his suit. The fabric sagged as though it had been pulled from the back of a closet. His jaw was rough with stubble, his nails ragged. He didn't look at her—yet—but resentment radiated from him like heat off asphalt.

The clerk called their case. Vanessa's throat went dry. She wished for water. For strength. For anything but this.

Her attorney leaned close. "Answer directly. Don't justify. Don't apologize. Let me handle the rest."

As if words could contain six years of strain, a Caribbean betrayal, and a child born from another man's blood.

The judge adjusted his glasses, scanning the file. "Ms. Pepper, you're requesting dissolution under the FAR Renewal Clause, correct?"

"Yes, Your Honor." Her voice trembled only slightly. "We renewed in 2025. But the marriage has... broken down. Irreparably."

The word lodged in her throat. *Irreparably.* So final—like the click of a lock sealing shut.

The judge turned. "Mr. Pepper, do you contest?"

August finally looked at her, his eyes sharp as glass. His lawyer nudged him, but his voice came out unfiltered.

"I don't want this. I didn't want it then, and I don't want it now. She's been halfway gone since Antigua."

The name sliced through her. *Antigua.* Spoken before in private, whispered behind closed doors. But here—echoing in the sterile air of the courtroom—it felt like a blade twisting. Her chest tightened.

The judge's brow furrowed. "Mr. Pepper, this court is not here to mediate past injuries. The question is whether the marriage remains viable under the statute."

"Viable?" August leaned forward, bitterness spilling like acid. "She decided it wasn't viable when she laid down with another man. But fine—stamp your papers. Call it official. I'm the only one who actually fought for this marriage."

Vanessa flinched, shame pressing into her ribs. For a moment, she could almost hear the waves outside the Antigua hotel, smell the salt in the air, taste the lie that had started everything. She had told herself it was escape, not betrayal. That she was only trying to remember who she was. But standing in this courtroom, she realized escape and ruin sometimes shared the same door.

Her attorney's voice cut through. "Your Honor, my client has already acknowledged the infidelity. This proceeding is about dissolution, not recrimination."

The judge nodded, though his gaze lingered on Vanessa a moment longer than she liked. The weight of his look said he had seen too many endings like this—too many people mistaking the ashes for proof of fire.

She looked down at her hands, at the faint white line where her wedding ring had lived. For the first time in years, she felt the space there breathe.

Her attorney rose, voice crisp and steady. "Your Honor, Mr. Pepper's remarks are irrelevant. The only question is whether continuing the renewal serves the interests of both parties—and their child."

Child. The word thickened the air.

The judge nodded. "Very well. Let's proceed to custody arrangements."

Vanessa's pulse quickened. This was where it mattered.

Her lawyer outlined their proposal: primary residence with Vanessa, alternating weekends with August, shared holidays. Standard. Fair. Predictable. She almost let herself exhale—until August leaned toward his lawyer and hissed, loud enough for her to hear,

"I want more than weekends. He's not even my blood, and I've done more for him than Seymour ever will."

The whisper seared. Vanessa's hands shook under the table. *Miles isn't a bargaining chip. He isn't proof of manhood.*

The judge looked up. "Mr. Pepper, do you contest the custody proposal?"

August rose slowly, pride and fury roughening his voice. "Yes, Your Honor. I want joint custody. Equal time. Miles knows me as his father. I won't be reduced to weekends like some babysitter."

Vanessa's chest seized. Equal custody meant disruption. Different schools, different rules, different homes. Miles pulled thin between them until something tore.

Her lawyer stood again, calm but unyielding. "With respect, Your Honor, joint custody would destabilize the child's routine. He has resided primarily with Ms. Pepper since birth. Continuity is essential."

The judge tapped his pen, the small sound echoing like a verdict. "Schedules will be reviewed. Shared legal custody is assumed. Physical custody to be determined."

August sat, eyes burning into her. His lips barely moved, but she caught it anyway: *You'll regret this.*

She forced her gaze forward. She would not flinch.

The rest blurred—division of debts, allocation of assets, sterile language dismantling a life. Each phrase landed like a hammer, flattening what they once built. When the gavel finally struck, Vanessa's hands trembled as she gathered her things.

August lingered, his stare heavy enough to bruise.

In the hallway, he caught up. The marble floor carried the sound of his shoes, sharp and deliberate.

"You think you won something in there?"

Her voice stayed steady, though her insides trembled.

"I didn't win," she said softly, letting a small tremor edge her words. "I survived."

His laugh was bitter, hollow enough to echo down the corridor.

"You're good at survival, Vanessa. But survival isn't love. And when Miles starts asking why, you'll have to tell him you walked away from the man who stayed."

Her mouth opened, then closed. There were no words that wouldn't cut them both. She wanted to tell him that leaving didn't mean she stopped loving him, that sometimes love itself could become a cage—but the truth caught somewhere between her throat and her heart.

He stepped closer, close enough for the scent of his cologne to sting her eyes. His voice dropped to a low, wounded growl. "You talk about drowning? You put me at the bottom of the ocean when you went to him. Don't expect me to forget it now."

Then he turned and walked away, shoulders stiff, footsteps ringing against the marble like a gavel that wouldn't stop striking.

Vanessa leaned against the wall. Her vision blurred. The urge to cry came hard and fast, but she swallowed it down, biting her lip until she tasted blood. Around her, the courthouse hummed with other endings— voices raised, papers shuffled, hearts rearranged—but all she could hear was his voice looping through her mind: *Survival isn't love.*

She pulled her phone from her bag, staring at the black screen until her reflection floated up. Thirty-nine years old. Mother. Professional. Survivor. The kind of woman who had learned to rebuild—but who still didn't know if she deserved more than endurance. Maybe she hadn't chosen freedom. Maybe she'd only chosen loneliness that looked better in daylight.

Her chest ached for Miles, who would grow up asking questions she couldn't yet answer. For herself, too, for the woman who had spent six years patching cracks with politeness and pretending that quiet meant peace.

Behind her, the courtroom doors banged shut like a final verdict. Yet inside her chest, nothing felt final at all.

At least she was no longer Mrs. Pepper.

She exhaled, slow and trembling. It wasn't victory. It wasn't peace. It was something smaller—something closer to the fragile beginning of freedom.

CHAPTER 3

The Ledger of One

Six months had passed. The courthouse doors had slammed shut like a verdict, and yet nothing inside Vanessa felt final. Time had kept its promise—it marched forward, relentless and indifferent.

The townhouse was hers. Two bedrooms stacked above a narrow living room, modest but enough. Lemon cleaner lingered faintly, mingling with the half-life of fresh paint. A small balcony caught sunlight just enough to keep her plants alive; the shed out back waited silently for Miles when he came over, promising a small kingdom just for him.

She ran her fingers along the smooth edge of the counter, noticing a faint scratch she hadn't seen before. Even this small imperfection reminded her that life, like furniture, could never stay perfectly polished.

Every bill, every rent payment, every key belonged to her. No shared ledger. No arguments about utilities or grocery lists. Just numbers, marching neatly in rows on her legal pad like soldiers awaiting orders. The fluorescent light hummed above, steady and loyal, keeping rhythm with her pulse.

"Mom?"

Miles's voice drifted from the dining table, crayons pressed too hard against paper until one snapped in two. He frowned, scrambling to fix it, whispering like the crayons had personally betrayed him.

"Yes, baby?" she asked, pencil still hovering above the ledger.

"Do we have enough for the field trip?"

He held up a crumpled flyer from Nevaeh—edges bent from his backpack—a $25 question resting in small, hopeful hands.

Vanessa blinked at the page in front of her, the neat

lines of expenses and due dates blurring slightly. She could almost hear the chorus of unseen numbers whispering back: rent, groceries, gas, balance due.

She smiled anyway. "We'll make it work."

She checked her calculations again. Twenty-five dollars. Tiny compared to the four figures she sent to Sallie Mae every month, yet her chest still clenched. She pressed her tongue against the roof of her mouth, her quiet ritual to keep panic from surfacing.

"Yes, baby, we have enough."

Relief bloomed bittersweet in his smile. Miles didn't know what *enough* meant. She did. Enough was survival—not comfort, not ease—just not drowning.

She rose and stirred the pot on the stove. The scent of chicken and rice mingled with onions and carrots, filling the narrow kitchen with a kind of humble warmth. She tasted a carrot—soft, sweet, slightly undercooked—and wondered if she would ever feel the satisfaction of abundance again.

Miles abandoned his crayons and dug in with the single-minded joy only children seemed to know. Watching him eat, she forced down a few bites herself, tasting mostly exhaustion and relief. Every choice, every mistake, every version of love she had tried to hold together had led her to this small table, this quiet evening, this fragile peace.

After dinner, she washed the dishes while Miles trailed behind, talking about dinosaurs and the zoo and a field trip that suddenly felt possible. The warm water ran over her hands, the hum of the faucet and the soft scrape of the sponge blending into a rhythm that steadied her heartbeat. The smell of soap, the clink of plates, the faint chatter of her son—each small sound anchored her, proof that she still belonged to the world.

Later, she tucked Miles into bed. He mumbled sleepily about dinosaurs, his small body curled around the stuffed turtle August had given him months ago. Vanessa lingered in the doorway, fingers brushing the edge of his blanket, watching the steady rise and fall of his chest.

"Goodnight, love," she whispered.

Back in the kitchen, the legal pad still lay open, rows of numbers glowing under the light like quiet accusations. She closed it and poured herself a small glass of wine, savoring the warmth as it slid down her throat.

Stepping onto the balcony, she leaned against the railing and let the night air find her. It smelled of faint smoke and distant rain, the kind that promised storms without delivering them. Below, the city hummed—a restless lullaby for those still awake and trying.

For the first time in months, she didn't feel crushed beneath the silence. She simply existed inside it. Breathing. Counting that, at least, as enough.

She raised her glass. "To the longest, hardest relationship I've ever had—myself," she whispered. "Not a Hallmark love story, but at least I'm still standing."

A faint scrape broke the stillness. Vanessa turned. Miles stood in the hallway, hair tousled from sleep, dragging his turtle by one limp leg. His small feet made soft sounds against the floor.

"Baby," she whispered, moving quickly toward him, "why are you up?"

"I was thirsty." He rubbed his eyes, then glanced at

the glass in her hand. "Is that juice?"

She gave a tired laugh. "No, sweetheart. Mommy's juice."

He wrinkled his nose. "Smells like socks."

Her smile faltered when his voice shrank to a whisper. "Where's Daddy sleeping tonight?"

The question hit her like a door closing. She set the glass aside and crouched, pulling him close. The turtle pressed awkwardly between them, but she didn't let go.

"Daddy has his own place now," she said softly. "Remember?"

"But why?" His lip trembled.

Because forgiveness had limits. Because silence had turned to rot. Because some homes crumble no matter how much you patch the walls. But she couldn't give him that truth.

"Sometimes grown-ups can't live in the same house anymore," she said instead, smoothing his hair. "But Daddy still loves you. That never changes."

"I want him here," Miles whispered into her shoulder.

Her chest tightened until she thought it might split.

She rocked him, slow and steady, as if motion alone could mend the break. When she carried him back to bed, his body was heavy in her arms, a weight made of everything she couldn't fix.

Later, she lingered at his doorway. The turtle had tumbled to the floor, his small hands curled against the blanket. She wanted to memorize that peace before morning unraveled it.

Back in the kitchen, the night felt wide and unsympathetic. The wineglass sat untouched on the balcony table. The city hummed beneath her, distant and unaware.

The law had written its ending, but August's shadow still wandered through her dreams. And in the hollow between midnight and morning, one question kept returning—if survival was hers now, would it ever be enough?

CHAPTER 4

Sundays in the Back Row

Vanessa parked three blocks from the church, just far enough to delay the inevitable. The morning air carried a faint scent of wet asphalt and early blooms, sharp and alive. For a moment, she let it fill her lungs, as if breathing it in might make her steadier.

Before leaving the house, she had dropped Miles at his friend's place. He hadn't looked up from the glowing console, barely waving goodbye. The sting of that lingered longer than she wanted to admit.

The engine ticked as it cooled, a metallic heartbeat fading under her hands. Her fingers tightened on the steering wheel—not from fear, not even anger, but from that quiet resistance the body feels when the mind has already decided what comes next. Five minutes to the church, five minutes to memory. It should have felt small, but she sat there, letting the weight of anticipation press against her chest.

Families passed along the sidewalk in choreographed ease—fathers adjusting bowties, mothers tugging jackets straight, children carrying Bibles nearly bigger than themselves. Their small talk rose and fell like a tide she no longer belonged to. Vanessa watched them the way one watches an old life through glass: familiar, unreachable.

Once, she had sat in the third row near the center aisle, her smile precise, her prayers rehearsed. Her faith had been fluent in the right words, her voice steady even when her heart wasn't. Back then, she knew exactly when to nod, when to whisper *amen*, when to seem whole.

Now, she pressed her thumb into the steering wheel, hard enough to leave a faint mark. The pressure grounded her in the present, even as thoughts uncoiled stubbornly inside her.

Finally, she opened the car door. The outside air felt heavier than the stillness she left behind, carrying hints of incense and the faint must of old carpet that drifted from the church steps. She locked the door and began walking, each step deliberate, a small defiance against the urge to turn back.

The bell tower chimed the quarter hour, its echo vibrating through her ribs and scattering across the quiet storefronts. The sound marked her pace, each note a reminder: the past doesn't stay buried just because you drive three blocks away.

Most people had already gone inside. A greeter in a navy blazer held the door open, smiling. "Good morning, welcome."

Vanessa nodded, eyes lowered, letting the church swallow her into its quiet order. The scent of polished wood and worn carpet wrapped around her like a familiar cloak, both comforting and heavy.

The sanctuary hadn't changed. Stained glass scattered sunlight into fractured color across the pews, and the organ hummed beneath it all—a low vibration that stirred something long dormant. She walked slowly down the side aisle, seeking a pocket of invisibility, and slipped into the last row near the back door. The leather seat was cold, worn by decades of restless bodies. It felt as if it had been waiting for her to return.

The announcements blurred together. Scripture readings rose and fell, practiced and even. Vanessa bowed her head, letting the words pass through her, pretending detachment. Then the hymn began.

"Come Thou Fount of Every Blessing…"

Her mouth opened before she meant it to. The sound startled her—thin, tentative, the ghost of a voice she hadn't used in months.

"Tune my heart to sing Thy grace…"

Her chest ached as the melody pulled at her. She followed as best she could, voice trembling, realizing what she had been avoiding: she was prone to wander. The admission stung. Tears dotted the page, turning the ink into faint bruises she quickly wiped away.

That's when she noticed him.

A man sat a few rows ahead, shoulders square,

posture still. Nothing showy, nothing meant to draw the eye—yet something about him radiated steadiness. A quiet confidence that filled the air around him without demanding it. Vanessa couldn't look away.

Was he married? Did he come every Sunday, like her? Or had he also parked blocks away, sitting in his car for a long time before deciding to walk through the doors?

The hymn ended. Books closed. Skirts rustled. Throats cleared.

Then the preacher's voice rose, smooth as a tide pulling against the hush. Words about wandering and coming home drifted through the sanctuary, gentle at first, then heavier with each verse. Every promise and warning pressed against the walls she'd built, touching corners of her she had tried not to feel.

Vanessa thought about slipping out—pretending her phone buzzed, letting the doors swing shut behind her. Her legs ached from holding still. Her fingers gripped the edge of the pew until her knuckles whitened. But something kept her rooted. Maybe it was defiance. Maybe it was the quiet steadiness of the man sitting a few rows ahead.

When the offering plate passed, she had nothing to give. Just silence, folded carefully into her lap, an invisible tithe she told herself would count.

The choir stood for the final hymn. Her throat tightened; her lips shaped the words, though no sound came. She studied the back of his head again—the evenness of his shoulders, the calm in his stillness—and felt an ache she didn't recognize.

When the benediction came, heads bowed. Voices rose in a soft Amen that trembled against the rafters. Vanessa stayed seated a moment longer, watching sunlight fade across the stained glass. Outwardly composed. Inwardly, still restless.

Her pulse refused to settle. Curiosity lingered, delicate and insistent. Who was he? And why did this small, ordinary moment feel like the beginning of something she had sworn she no longer needed?

CHAPTER 5

The Man Who Listens

The lobby was louder than she remembered. Voices ricocheted off one another, rising and falling in uneven rhythm, a dozen conversations blending into a persistent hum. From the far side of the room came a burst of laughter, bright and buoyant, slicing through the noise like sunlight breaking through clouds. Vanessa's shoulders tensed at the sound, though no one else seemed to notice.

Two children darted past her, their shoes squeaking against the polished floorboards, paper airplanes raised like tiny swords in a secret duel. The ink-stained wings fluttered with each motion, and behind them, their parents called after them, voices fraying with a mixture of apology and command. Near the nursery doors, a baby cried, the sharp wail swallowed by the greater din, until it became part of the steady tide of noise pressing against Vanessa's ribs.

She lingered by the bulletin board, her fingers brushing the edges of the pinned flyers. The clutter grounded her—something solid amid the blur of movement. Corners of posters curled with age: a youth retreat, a potluck sign-up, a prayer breakfast notice. Even the sagging pin on a yellowed choir rehearsal sheet seemed to whisper of quiet endurance. She traced the folds and creases with her eyes, counting imperfections, building a small refuge in the act of noticing.

One more minute, she told herself. Just one more, and she could leave. Her body rehearsed the motion before her mind allowed it.

Then he appeared—a shape cutting through the crowd and into her path, close enough that the faint aroma of coffee drifted between them. The man from the sanctuary. He seemed taller here, steadier somehow, the same quiet confidence that had filled the space when he spoke. The light from the overhead fixtures touched his dark hair, softening the edges.

He didn't speak right away. His eyes searched hers, not demanding, only waiting. The murmur of the lobby faded at the edges, the way sound recedes before a storm. Vanessa felt the old tension coil in her shoulders again, the push to retreat warring with something unfamiliar—something almost like relief.

"Vanessa," he said finally, his voice a low, even current.

She nodded, though her throat tightened too much to answer. The sound of her name from him carried weight, a recognition she hadn't realized she was waiting for.

For a heartbeat, they stood in the midst of the noise and motion, neither moving, the air between them threaded with the faint scent of coffee and something gentler—patience, maybe.

And then she remembered to breathe.

"Oh, sorry," she said, stepping back. Her voice

sounded thin even to her own ears.

"It's alright," he said, glancing around briefly before returning his gaze to hers. "Not much of a traffic pattern here."

Vanessa nodded, instinctively angling toward the door. But something in his calm voice paused her motion.

"You can have one of these," he said, gesturing toward the coffee table. "The coffee's terrible, though. Cinnamon rolls go first."

She blinked, caught off guard by the humor, and a small laugh escaped—light and unexpected, cutting through the tight coil of nerves in her chest.

They collided briefly with another passerby, a book slipping from his pocket. Instinctively, Vanessa bent to pick it up. *The Cost of Discipleship*, she read, feeling the weight of the paper and the quiet gravity of his choice to carry it.

He reached for it, then paused mid-motion. "Keep it," he said softly.

Vanessa hesitated, the faint stirrings of trust and curiosity rising like warmth beneath her ribs. "Alright," she whispered. "Thank you."

He smiled, small and private, as though the gesture said everything without words. Then he turned away, coffee cup steady, sunlight catching his shoulders as the summer air swallowed him.

Vanessa stood for a moment, thumb tracing the spine of the book. A quiet warmth spread through her chest—the first gift she had accepted in months without judgment, without instruction.

CHAPTER 6

Conversations After Amen

Sunday mornings still startled Vanessa with their brightness. The streets outside her apartment were half empty, sun-washed and quiet, as though the city had decided to forgive itself for the week. She almost convinced herself to stay home—make coffee, fold the laundry, pretend she wasn't thinking about him. Almost.

Her hand hovered over the gearshift longer than necessary. "It's just church," she muttered, half to herself, half to the dashboard. "Not jury duty." The car offered no reassurance, only the faint rattle of the A/C that smelled faintly of crayons from Miles's last coloring spree.

She drove slowly, savoring the red lights as if the universe were giving her permission to pause, to reconsider. At one stop, she caught sight of a man on the corner juggling three rolls of toilet paper with alarming confidence. Vanessa laughed out loud—the kind of surprised, reluctant laugh that left a warmth in her chest. "If he can do that in public," she murmured, "I can sit through one sermon."

By the time the church steeple peeked above the treeline, her nerves had returned, fluttering sharp as moth wings. She circled the block once before finally parking two blocks away beneath an elm tree. The morning air smelled of sun-warmed leaves and distant pavement, carrying the faint hum of a city waking up. She let it linger, inhaling the quiet, before shutting off the engine.

The book rested in her lap, spine creased, edges folded. She hadn't planned to return it today. She hadn't finished it either, though the underlined lines whispered across her mind, refusing to let her go. Each mark felt like a small tether, binding her to a thought, a feeling, and, unbidden, to him.

Part of her hoped he wouldn't be there—it would be safer, simpler, less complicated. But a braver part of her wanted to see him again, even if only for a fleeting acknowledgment, a quiet nod that could speak volumes without words.

Inside, the sanctuary felt familiar and strange all at once. The back pew embraced her like a memory she couldn't quite name, holding her still while the room pulsed with life. Voices rose and fell, footsteps echoed, the swell of the organ filling the air with something both commanding and gentle. She kept the book in her hands, thumb tracing the spine, as if the paper itself offered a quiet sanctuary.

She settled in, letting the murmurs wash over her, each sound folding into the next, until she became part of it without noticing. Every creak of the pew, every rustle of programs, every soft cough and whispered greeting seemed to echo inside her, stirring a nervous anticipation she hadn't named.

A sunbeam cut through the stained-glass windows, painting the floor in fractured color. Vanessa watched it move, chasing the patterns across the wooden boards, and felt a flicker of calm. She imagined him walking in, coffee cup in hand, a small smile playing on his lips, and she allowed herself a private hope that maybe today, the conversation would come easier.

The book in her lap felt heavier now, as if it carried not just words but a promise of connection, of understanding. And for the first time in a long while, she let herself believe that it might be more than just a fleeting moment—that the quiet warmth that had begun to settle in her chest could linger.

There he was. Same seat, same calm presence, shoulders square, hands loosely clasped. Vanessa looked away, heart hammering, letting the ritual of service wash over her. The scripture readings pressed gently against her chest, steady and grounding. The benediction ended; the crowd began to drift toward the lobby. Vanessa counted her breaths, letting the emptying room slow her pulse before she moved.

He stood by the coffee table, stirring cream into a cup, the spoon balanced at the edge. She stepped closer, tightening her grip on the book, each heartbeat echoing in her ears.

"Oh, sorry," she said, stepping back. Her voice sounded thin even to her own ears.

"It's alright," he said, glancing around briefly before returning his gaze to hers. "Not much of a traffic pattern here."

"You underlined page seventy-four," she said softly, almost afraid the words would vanish before he heard.

He looked up, a faint smile brushing his mouth. "So did you."

The tension in her shoulders eased slightly. She exhaled, feeling the quiet permission in his acknowledgment, the ease of being seen without explanation. "That's where it started to make sense," she whispered.

He nodded gently. No questions. No pressure. Just presence. Silence held them together for a few moments, a private bubble amid the soft hum of the lobby.

"You can have one of these," he said, gesturing toward the coffee table. "The coffee's terrible, though. Cinnamon rolls go first."

She blinked, caught off guard by the humor, and a small laugh escaped—light and unexpected, cutting through the tight coil of nerves in her chest.

They collided briefly with another passerby, a book slipping from his pocket. Instinctively, Vanessa bent to pick it up. *The Cost of Discipleship*, she read, feeling the weight of the paper and the quiet gravity of his choice to carry it.

He reached for it, then paused mid-motion. "Keep it," he said softly.

Vanessa hesitated, the faint stirrings of trust and curiosity rising like warmth beneath her ribs. "Alright," she whispered. "Thank you."

He smiled, small and private, as though the gesture said everything without words. Then he turned away, coffee cup steady, sunlight catching his shoulders as the summer air swallowed him.

Vanessa stood for a moment, thumb tracing the spine of the book. A quiet warmth spread through her chest—the first gift she had accepted in months without judgment, without instruction.

"You hungry?" he asked suddenly, glancing toward

the door.

She shook her head, hesitating. "I should probably head home."

"Fair enough," he said.

Her fingers tapped the spine of the book. "I'll walk with you. Just to the lot," she added impulsively, as if the motion itself gave her courage.

"Alright," he replied, his voice steady, reassuring.

The sun was warm, gentle, dappling the sidewalk through shifting leaves. Their steps fell into rhythm, soft and deliberate. Vanessa let herself notice—the scrape of shoes against asphalt, the rustle of leaves above, the distant echo of children's laughter. She pictured Miles, safe and laughing, steadying her in memory.

"You don't talk like most people here," she said finally, the words spilling softly between them.

"I don't know if that's a compliment," he said.

"It is," she assured him, a small smile lifting her lips. "There's no performance in you."

A quiet truth passed between them. No explanations, no need for embellishment—just the weight of small, honest fragments, enough to leave space for thought and feeling.

They reached her car. She shifted the book in her hands, tracing the cover as if memorizing it all over again. "You said to keep it."

"I did," he said simply. "I've lived it more than twice."

A laugh, startled and honest, slipped from her lips. In that moment, she understood: conversations could leave her fuller, not empty, and connection could arrive in small, patient fragments.

Vanessa watched him walk away, the sunlight catching the angle of his shoulders, the soft sway of his steps carrying him out of sight. The warmth of their conversation lingered in her chest, a quiet pulse she hadn't expected but welcomed.

She opened the car door and slid in, the leather cool beneath her fingers. The book rested on her lap, heavier now, as if it carried not only words but a memory of presence, of being seen without judgment. Vanessa traced the spine again, letting herself imagine him returning, speaking simply, offering space in the midst of noise and expectation.

The city hummed around her, distant yet familiar. A breeze stirred, lifting leaves along the curb. She breathed in, steady and deliberate, noticing the small details—the scent of asphalt warmed by the sun, the chirp of a bird in a nearby tree, the echo of her own heartbeat—and felt a surprising sense of calm.

For the first time in months, she allowed herself to hope, quietly and without fanfare, that connection could exist in fragments, that presence could be enough. She turned the key in the ignition, the engine purring to life, and carried the memory with her— small, steady, and luminous, like sunlight through stained glass.

CHAPTER 7

The Space Between Us

It had been a month since their first real coffee date, but Vanessa still remembered the way Ethan had leaned in that day, elbows planted on the café table as if he had nowhere else to be. The café itself had been loud—espresso machine hissing, someone's phone buzzing at the next table, chairs scraping across the floor—but none of it seemed to reach him. He looked at her as if silence had wrapped around only them.

She had been talking about something ordinary, barely worth mentioning: how Miles had taken apart his toy car just to see if it would run without wheels. Yet the way Ethan's eyes caught hers, steady and warm, made her feel as if she had said something extraordinary. It was the kind of attention she hadn't felt in years—the kind that didn't just listen but truly received, absorbing the words and the quiet weight behind them.

Things had shifted since then, quietly at first, then all at once. They saw each other nearly every day now, folding into each other's rhythms like it had been rehearsed. Some nights she cooked, garlic sizzling in olive oil while Ethan leaned against the counter, sleeves rolled up, recounting some absurd moment from work. Other nights he arrived with takeout: cartons of noodles, tacos wrapped in foil, fried chicken that made Miles hum happily between bites. They ate at the table, on the couch, wherever felt right.

Vanessa found herself laughing more, not at anything monumental but at little things—the way Ethan exaggerated a story, the way Miles interrupted to add his own version, the way Ethan let himself be corrected by a six-year-old with all the gravity of a man receiving expert advice. In those moments, she felt a quiet contentment, the kind that settled in her chest and stayed there long after the laughter faded.

At first, she had worried about the invitation—the quiet exposure of letting someone new witness the real parts of her life. The jelly stains on the counters, the endless parade of socks without matches, the sharp reality that being a mother meant chaos and not much mystery. She had thought he might stiffen at the mess, or keep his distance when Miles clung too tightly. Instead, Ethan stepped into it like he belonged, moving with a natural ease, noticing her and her son without judgment, without pretense.

Some evenings, after Miles was asleep, Vanessa would linger in the living room, the quiet hum of the city outside mingling with the faint aroma of leftover takeout. She would watch Ethan in the kitchen, chopping vegetables or rinsing dishes, and marvel at the simple intimacy of it. It wasn't fireworks or declarations. It was presence. It was listening. It was showing up again and again. And somehow, in that consistency, Vanessa found herself letting down walls she hadn't realized were still standing.

On Saturday morning, he showed up with

49

pancakes from the diner down the street, balancing the bag awkwardly because Miles had already launched himself into his arms. Ethan lifted the boy easily, setting him on his shoulders, moving through the hallway as if it were the most natural thing in the world. Vanessa stood in the kitchen doorway, watching them, her hands damp from dishwater. The sight caught her in the chest—too familiar and too impossible all at once.

And Vanessa? She started to breathe again. Subtle at first, just a loosening in her ribs, but then stronger, like remembering a song she'd once loved.

The ordinary became extraordinary in its steadiness. Ethan rinsing cereal bowls without being asked. Ethan kneeling on the floor to help Miles with a Lego spaceship, squinting as though its construction were a matter of national security. Ethan brushing Vanessa's wrist dry after water splashed up from the sink, his thumb lingering as though drying her hand were a privilege. Healing, she realized, sometimes came not in thunder but in these small offerings.

They kissed often now—doorframe kisses, kitchen

kisses, those quick touches stolen between dishes and bedtime stories. They kissed like people who knew what it was to go without. It wasn't only heat—it was relief, restoration, the kind of return that made her believe in softness again.

One evening, after dinner and bedtime routines, the apartment sank into quiet. The walls seemed closer, the light softer, the air thicker with waiting. Vanessa stood at the counter, robe loose around her, the hum of the kettle filling the silence. She turned when she felt him in the doorway. Ethan leaned there, watching her, and the world seemed to narrow to just that look.

"Coffee?" she asked, voice low.

He shook his head, smiling. "Not unless you want me up all night lecturing about compound interest."

Her laugh was nervous but real. It broke the hush, and it was enough to close the distance between them.

The kiss wasn't new, but tonight it carried a weight that made everything else vanish. His hand cupped her face, thumb tracing her cheekbone, while her fingers clenched his shirt, drawing him closer. Every movement was urgent, deliberate, as if they were being pulled together by something invisible yet undeniable.

Their mouths deepened, hunger rising in every brush of tongue and uneven breath. He traced her jaw, her neck, the tender spot beneath her ear, and she trembled, whispering his name, letting it shatter the quiet.

This was no longer tentative or searching. Restraint had given way to need. Heat pooled between them, raw and unhidden. She felt him memorize her with every touch, while she clung to him, braver than she had dared in months. Her chest pressed against his, every gasp carrying the longing they had starved for too long.

They stumbled toward the couch, drawn by instinct rather than planning. Her knees hit the cushions, and she let herself fall, pulling him down with her. His hands sought the belt of her robe, sliding it open. She did not shy away. She wanted him to see her, to know the truth of her desire.

His eyes darkened with need, and his mouth traced the line of her jaw, down her throat, lingering at the hollow of her chest. His hands mapped her curves, igniting heat into her skin, and she answered in breathless moans and urgent whimpers.

Her own hands roamed, tugging at his clothes, peeling away layer after layer until nothing separated them. Skin pressed to skin, their kisses grew harder, deeper, each touch a wordless confession. When he pressed against her, her body arched, lips parted, eyes locking with his in a silent promise.

He moved with measured intensity, every thrust drawing cries and gasps from both of them. Her legs wrapped around him, arms threading around his neck, pulling him closer, urging him forward. There were no words left, only the rhythm of bodies meeting, of desire spilling over, unstoppable and all-consuming.

In the press of their closeness, the world beyond them ceased to exist. Every heartbeat, every tremor of skin, every gasp of air carried them higher, carried them together, until the ache and the heat became something sacred—an unspoken devotion written in touch, in moans, in the fevered press of lips and bodies finally, gloriously, freed.

Even when the first wave of release tore through them, they didn't pause. Still joined, still hungry, they moved again, chasing the high, losing themselves in each other until time blurred and the room seemed to spin.

Soft laughter threaded through kisses in the aftermath, fingertips tracing skin where fevered hands had just been. Their need flared again and again, insistent and unrelenting, until the fire between them softened into something deeper, steadier—kisses that carried quiet promises, touches that whispered of belonging.

Eventually, exhaustion came, but it wasn't empty. It was the sweet stillness of being utterly, completely fulfilled. Vanessa lay against his chest, letting the steady beat of his heart ground her, his hand moving in slow, idle circles down her back.

"I'm not your rescue," he murmured, voice low, trembling just enough to reach her.

"I know," she replied, certain. "But you're the first thing that's felt alive in a long time."

He pressed a kiss to her forehead, lingering before brushing his lips to hers again—slow, deliberate, like a vow renewed. She closed her eyes, inhaling the quiet intimacy, her body still alive with their closeness.

For the first time in years, she didn't brace for an ending. She leaned fully into a beginning.

Piece by piece, breath by breath, heartbeat by heartbeat, she rose—

and this time, she wasn't alone.

CHAPTER 8

Grace Without Fireworks

Morning light softened the apartment, slipping through the thin curtains in warm, golden stripes. Vanessa stirred, noticing how naturally her body felt, the ease of waking with Ethan's arm draped over her waist. His breathing was steady and warm against the back of her neck. For a long moment, she didn't move. She simply existed in the quiet, savoring a peace that felt almost too rare to be real.

The soft creak of small footsteps down the hall broke the stillness. Miles appeared in the doorway, hair wild, pajama shirt twisted from sleep. His eyes widened at the sight of Ethan, at his mother wrapped in someone else's embrace.

"Mom?" he asked softly, rubbing his eyes.

Ethan stirred, sitting up slowly, careful not to startle him. "Morning, buddy," he said, voice husky from sleep.

Miles hesitated for only a heartbeat before padding over and climbing onto the edge of the bed as if it were the most natural thing in the world. Ethan shifted slightly to make room, one hand resting steady on the boy's back.

"Want pancakes?" Ethan asked, a half-smile tugging at his lips. Then—just a flicker—he glanced at Vanessa, as if checking whether he'd said the right thing.

Miles's face lit up instantly. "With chocolate chips?"

Vanessa laughed softly, leaning against Ethan's shoulder. The sound felt like sunlight spilling over the two of them, warming the little world of the room. Ethan's eyes met hers, a quiet acknowledgment passing between them—a shared promise that some moments, small and ordinary, were enough.

"Obviously," Ethan said, his grin returning, easy

and natural.

Vanessa watched them, throat tight, chest full. She had thought last night was the miracle—the heat, the closeness, the way her body had remembered joy. But maybe this was the real gift: the effortless laughter of her son, the gentle way Ethan folded into their morning, the quiet belonging of the three of them in the same frame of golden light.

For the first time in a very long time, the future didn't feel like something to fear. It felt like something she might actually be ready to meet.

***

Later that evening, when the babysitter arrived, Vanessa still carried that warmth with her, a soft glow she couldn't quite shake.

Nevaeh stepped through the door—young, radiant, and brimming with cheerful energy. She was dressed in denim and a confident smile, her backpack slung casually over one shoulder, the kind of effortless presence that seemed to brighten a room simply by being in it.

"Hey, Ms. Pepper!" she chirped. "Miles and I are gonna finish that volcano project tonight."

Vanessa felt her shoulders loosen slightly, as they always did when Nevaeh came around. The girl had a way of making life feel simpler, like the heavy parts of adulthood could wait until tomorrow.

"Thanks for coming, Nevaeh," Vanessa said warmly, stepping aside. "Snacks are on the counter. You know the drill."

"Got it!" Nevaeh grinned, already toeing off her sneakers before rushing down the hallway toward Miles's room. Her laughter trailed after her, light and infectious. Vanessa turned back just in time to catch Ethan smiling politely, his expression quiet, steady. He was already halfway out the door, car keys dangling from one hand.

"I'll meet you in the car, honey," he called to Vanessa, adding a quick wink that made her heart lift just a little higher.

Vanessa lingered for a moment in the doorway, watching the small world she loved so fiercely—her son, Ethan, and the ordinary magic of a home that felt alive with warmth. For once, the chaos and noise of life seemed not to matter, and she let herself just breathe, letting the quiet grace of the evening settle around her like a soft, unspoken promise.

She nodded, moving toward the closet for her coat. But when she reached for her sleeve, something caught her eye—the front door hadn't fully closed. It was cracked open just enough for sound to slip through. And sound did. Ethan's voice drifted back through the gap, easy and amused.

"Yeah, man… the babysitter's here. You should see her. Perfect for you. Her name's Nevaeh—heaven spelled backwards. And her tits? Man, they're heavenly too."

Vanessa froze. The casualness, the smirk in his tone—it sent a jolt down her spine before her mind could catch up. For a heartbeat, she stood perfectly still, hands pressed against the wall. Something inside her shifted, like a fault line cracking open.

She drew a steadying breath and moved toward the entryway, fingers brushing the table as she picked up her keys. The metal was cool against her palm. Ethan, mid-laugh, glanced back, caught off guard. The phone slipped slightly lower against his ear.

"Who are you talking to?" she asked, her voice steady, calm on the surface, though heat pooled beneath her ribs.

He blinked, hesitation flickering across his face. Then the easy grin slid back into place. "My brother," he said. "I thought he might be perfect for Nevaeh."

Vanessa stepped fully onto the porch, keeping her gaze locked on him. "What makes you think that?"

The grin faltered, tension threading his jaw. "She's cute. Friendly. Around his age."

Her eyes didn't waver. "You didn't mention that," she said softly. "You mentioned her body. Not her character. Not how she handles my son like a pro. You reduced her to tits."

Silence pressed against them like a living thing. Ethan's throat worked as he swallowed, his free hand dropping into his pocket.

"I'm sorry," he said finally, the weight in his voice unguarded. "That was careless."

Vanessa studied him, her heart still racing, a mix of frustration and disbelief swirling inside her. She didn't answer right away, letting the quiet stretch between them—letting him feel it, letting herself feel it.

For a flash, Vanessa almost let it slide. Almost told herself it was just a stupid slip, not worth derailing the night. The temptation tugged hard—after all, hadn't she wanted this? A man who made pancakes, who winked at her across rooms, who made mornings feel like possibility.

But she pushed the thought down, firm. "It wasn't just careless," she said. "It was thoughtless. And not at all like the man who said he wanted to build something respectful with me."

His shoulders dipped, the grin gone now. "You're right."

"I won't let you turn Nevaeh—or me—into an afterthought," Vanessa added, her tone sharper, cutting clean through the night air.

Ethan's gaze fell, eyes shadowed. "I get it. I do."

"Then show me," she said quietly. "Because words are easy. Respect isn't."

The space between them felt taut, like a rope pulled to its breaking point, every second holding a weight neither of them could ignore.

"I'll do better," Ethan said finally, voice low, stripped of charm, bare in a way that made the honesty sting.

Vanessa didn't reply. She turned slightly, pulling the front door closed with deliberate care. The click of the latch sounded louder than it should have—sharp, final, a punctuation to what had passed.

***

The drive was quiet, the hum of the engine filling the spaces where words might have been. Ethan cleared his throat once. "Do you want to talk about it now," he asked cautiously, "or later?"

Vanessa's eyes stayed on the passing blur of streetlights. "There's nothing more to explain. I told you what mattered."

He nodded, fingers tightening on the wheel. When they parked, he hesitated. "We don't have to go in. We can head home, order takeout."

"I'll go in," she said, her voice steady, but not forgiving. "But I don't want to pretend it didn't happen."

"I wouldn't ask you to," he said, and the words hung between them, quiet but heavy—an acknowledgment of the moment, of the trust they were both still learning to navigate.

Inside, the restaurant buzzed with the soft clinking of glassware and low chatter. They slid into a booth, menus placed between them. A waitress brought water; condensation ran down the glasses. Vanessa wrapped her hands around hers, grounding herself in the chill.

"You want to split something?" Ethan asked gently.

"I'll order for myself." Her voice was even, not defensive—just clear.

He nodded.

When the waitress left with their orders, Ethan leaned forward, elbows on the table. "I don't want to make excuses," he said. "That joke—it wasn't about Nevaeh. It was me being lazy, careless. It came out of my mouth too easily. That scares me."

Vanessa tilted her head, letting the silence stretch,

feeling the weight of it settle between them.

"It's not who I want to be," he continued, quieter now. "Not with you. Not with Miles. But if I'm not paying attention—old habits creep in. And that's not the man I want to show you."

She didn't rescue him with reassurance. Instead, she sipped her water, the chill pressing faintly against her chest, a reminder of the clarity she wanted to hold onto.

Finally, she spoke. "Then what you showed me tonight is that you still have work to do. And I need to see that work. Not hear it."

Ethan nodded once. "Fair."

The waitress dropped off a basket of bread. Vanessa broke one open, the warmth against her fingertips a quiet comfort. Dignity, she reminded herself, often lived in the smallest gestures.

"You're not going to let me slide on this, are you?" Ethan asked.

"No," she said simply.

A faint smile ghosted across his lips—not joy, but recognition. "Good. I don't deserve sliding."

They ate quietly after that, the silence stretching not as emptiness but as expectation. He had ground to prove. She had ground to hold.

When they stepped back into the night air, Vanessa's steps were steady, keys cool in her hand. Ethan walked beside her, quieter than usual. She knew she hadn't ended anything tonight. But she also knew she hadn't bent.

And that, more than anything, felt like survival.

CHAPTER 9

Host Of August

It happened on a Thursday, one of those quiet, indistinct days that blur together.

Vanessa was in the dining room, a laundry basket tipped open beside her. The window was cracked just enough to let in the faint hum of traffic and the damp smell of asphalt from an earlier rain. Her sleeves were rolled up, hair twisted into a knot that had already loosened. She was trying, really trying, to fold the clothes as if it mattered.

On the counter, a half-finished smoothie sat sweating into a ring on the wood. The purple mixture had begun to separate—dark at the bottom, pale at the top.

The buzz of her phone cut through the stillness, lighting the counter with a faint glow that made the condensation shimmer. She had a shirt in her hands—Miles's, something small and soft, the kind of fabric that clung to her palms when it was fresh from the dryer. She smoothed it flat against the table, pressed the sleeves inward, lining up the edges with the same deliberate care she'd used the night before buttering bread at the restaurant.

The repetition steadied her, gave her hands something to do while her mind tried to find balance.

Then the vibration came again.

Vanessa wiped her damp hands on her leggings and turned toward the screen. The name on the display stopped her breath.

AUGUST.

Her pulse jumped hard, a quick thud behind her ears. Before she could talk herself out of it, she tapped the notification with trembling fingers.

The text read:

Hey. Didn't think I'd ever text you again, but… I've been thinking about you.

The words were plain. No apology, no grand plea—just a line. Short enough to sound casual, sharp enough to pierce through the fragile calm of her day.

Her stomach tightened, as if the ground beneath her had tilted slightly.

It had been over a year since they'd spoken like adults. He still saw Miles on his weekends, but between them—silence. Twelve full months of it.

The details of August had dulled around the edges: the exact timbre of his laugh, the cadence of his walk, the way his hand moved when he was trying to make a point. Those fragments had faded, like photographs left too long in the sun—still visible, but pale, fragile, almost gone.

Her hand clenched tighter around the phone. The message wasn't a reunion. It felt like a knock on a door she had once bricked over with both hands. Her thumb hovered above the keyboard. She imagined typing something final, something that would close the door forever, but her fingers never moved.

Instead, she set the phone face down on the counter, the black screen swallowing his name.

She tried to return to the laundry. She picked up another shirt, one of her own this time, and folded it along its seams. The motion was steady, mechanical. The room felt dimmer, though the same light streamed through the window as before.

Her thoughts refused to stay still. They skittered in small, sharp loops.

Why now?

What does he want?

Does he want anything at all?

Maybe it was nothing.

Maybe it was everything.

She thought about telling Ethan that night when he brought dinner over, when he smiled at her across the table as Miles chattered between them. She thought about telling him again when he leaned in to kiss her before leaving, his breath soft against her cheek.

But she didn't. The words stayed locked in her chest, beating hard against her ribs.

Ethan noticed the change, though neither of them spoke about it. The silence between them started small—so small she almost convinced herself it wasn't there. But it began to show up in quiet places. In her phone. In the pauses between her replies.

Where she once texted him back in minutes, sometimes seconds, she now let hours pass. She would see his name light up her screen and think, *I'll answer after this chore. After I put Miles to bed. After I feel less crowded in my own head.*

And sometimes, by the time she finally wrote back, she realized she had forgotten what he had even asked.

He never confronted her. Never asked what was wrong. Ethan wasn't the type to send question marks in a row, the way August used to whenever she hesitated too long. He didn't press. He waited.

And somehow, his patience unsettled her even more.

The silence crept into the mornings too. At the doorway, when he left, the goodbye kisses grew shorter. She kept telling herself she wasn't pulling away. What she was doing, she thought, was turning over every stone inside her chest, studying each one. The pace of things. The closeness. The way she had let Ethan into her life without pausing to check the locks

71

she had once sworn to guard.

At night, when the house settled into stillness and Miles slept with his door cracked just enough for her to hear his soft breaths, she lay awake with those stones heavy in her hands. Sometimes the weight felt unbearable. Sometimes she wondered if she had imagined it all.

She remembered the promises she made to herself after August. That she would be careful. That she would breathe before opening the door to anyone new. That she would build her walls high, thick enough to protect not only herself but Miles too.

And then Ethan had come, quiet and steady, with a kind of gentleness she hadn't known how to refuse. Somehow he was inside before she realized the locks had turned. The thought unsettled her.

Was it safety, or carelessness?

Was she lucky, or was she reckless?

The questions lingered, clinging to her like humidity that refused to lift.

Sometimes his restraint made her want to cry. Other times it made her ache with guilt.

On Sunday, he stopped by to drop off a book for Miles. It wasn't a special occasion, just a small, thoughtful gesture. He stood on the front step with it tucked under his arm, the late afternoon light catching the edge of his hair and laying a stripe of gold across his shoulders.

Vanessa opened the door and leaned against the frame. Her arms folded tight across her chest, holding her together like a seam on the verge of splitting.

Ethan smiled and lifted the book slightly. "Thought Miles might like this one."

She should have said thank you. She should have let him in, offered him water, pretended nothing had shifted inside her. Instead, she stood frozen in the doorway, the weight of her own silence pressing hard against her ribs. Her pulse was louder than the passing cars, louder than her thoughts.

She knew she couldn't keep carrying the secret. It had already grown sharp enough to bruise.

The words slipped out of her before she could stop them. "I got a message," she said.

Ethan's expression didn't change right away. He

stayed where he was, his gaze steady on her face, the quiet between them drawn tight like a wire.

Her breath came uneven. "From someone I used to care about. Someone who left things messy."

The confession hung there, fragile and uncertain. The words sounded smaller out loud than they had in her head, like something that had lost its power the moment it met air.

Ethan nodded slowly. His face was unreadable but not unkind. "You don't owe me anything," he said softly. "But if it's sitting in your chest, maybe don't let it sit there alone."

His voice was gentle, and that gentleness cut deeper than anger ever could.

The simplicity of it startled her. He wasn't prying. He wasn't demanding answers. He was just offering to share the weight.

For a moment, she couldn't breathe. Most men she had known—most men she had trusted—would have turned that message into a fight, or a guilt trip, or a weapon to use later when the balance of power tilted. But Ethan just stood there, hands in his jacket pockets, his voice calm, his eyes steady. Nothing about her confession seemed to threaten him.

She blinked hard. Her throat ached, thick with something she couldn't name. She didn't know whether his steadiness was a comfort or another burden she wasn't strong enough to carry.

The words tumbled out before she could stop them. "I just..." She faltered, her voice catching. Her nails pressed into her arms where they were crossed, sharp enough to leave little crescents on her skin. "I feel like I rushed into this with you. Like I didn't stop to breathe."

The admission lingered in the air, trembling like a fragile thread. Once it escaped, she wanted it back. She wanted to tuck it deep inside her chest where no one could see it, where it couldn't be misunderstood.

Ethan didn't rush to fill the silence. He didn't reach for her or try to fix what she had said. He just stood there, his face still, caught in the thin weave of light and shadow from the porch. His jaw tightened once, a flicker of effort to keep his first reaction from surfacing.

When he finally spoke, his voice was quiet and sure. "I can step back," he said. The words came slowly, each one chosen with care. "If you need to take a breath."

She swallowed hard. "Just a breath," she said. "Not a goodbye."

His reply came softly. "Okay."

That was all. No argument. No punishment. Just grace.

The simplicity of it stunned her more than anger ever could have. Ethan adjusted his jacket and stepped down from the porch. His movements were unhurried, measured, as if he understood that leaving gently was a kind of love too. Vanessa stayed where she was, arms still crossed, holding herself together with a grip that had begun to ache.

The late afternoon light bent across the street, tracing a faint gold line along his shoulders and the back of his neck. She thought of all the evenings he had stood in that same spot before, waving as he left, promising to call later. Each memory rose like smoke, thin and ungraspable.

Halfway to the car, he stopped. His voice carried

across the distance between them, calm and even. "You know," he said, "even if this doesn't work out, you still deserve good love. Just don't let ghosts teach you otherwise."

The words landed like a touch against her skin, soft but piercing. Her hand tightened around the doorframe, the wood pressing into her palm as her heart thudded against her ribs.

By the time she blinked, he was moving again. The car door closed with a muted click. The engine started, its quiet hum blending with the stillness of the street. The taillights glowed briefly before disappearing around the corner.

Then the quiet returned.

The world outside looked unchanged—the trees, the pavement, the pale wash of light—but everything inside her felt rearranged. Gratitude tangled with confusion. A strange tenderness filled her chest, mingled with the ache of something fragile she wasn't sure how to name.

She closed the door slowly, her fingers brushing the cool metal of the lock. The sound of it sliding into place echoed through the empty house, steady and final. But in her heart, nothing felt closed at all.

CHAPTER 10

Boundaries & Blueprints

Miles crouched low in the mulch, his tongue peeking out in concentration as both hands worked to steady a crooked twig against the little pile he had already built. His "bridge," as he called it, sagged in the middle and threatened to collapse. He frowned, adjusted the base with quick fingers, and balanced two pebbles on top as though daring the world to prove him wrong. It wasn't even. It wasn't neat. But it stood. And in his six-year-old world, standing was everything.

Vanessa sat on the bench a few yards away, cradling a paper cup of coffee between her palms. The lid had softened from the steam, and her fingers traced its edges as if learning them by heart. Her phone rested facedown beside her, its black screen catching bits of weak Saturday sunlight. She had promised herself—no emails today. Not on a Saturday. It should have been easy, but the habit itched at the back of her mind, small and persistent as a mosquito. Still, she resisted. Miles deserved her eyes, not her distracted nods.

Across the playground, Anthone leaned against the iron fence, somehow managing to look like he'd wandered out of a magazine shoot and into the park by mistake. His navy coat was crisp, the dark fabric catching faint light each time he shifted. Designer sunglasses hid his eyes, though the day was hardly bright. He crossed one ankle over the other, arms folded loosely across his chest. Nothing about him ever looked accidental. Even the angle of his lean, that slight backward tilt with his chin lifted, seemed arranged with quiet precision.

He watched Miles with a small smile, the kind that seemed genuine at first glance yet never touched the space behind his lenses.

Vanessa glanced up at him now and then, unsure if

she wanted him here or if she had only agreed because it felt simpler than arguing. The two of them had a rhythm, awkward but familiar, built from years of almost understanding each other. She sipped her coffee and tried to focus on her son's laughter, but the sound of Anthone's slow exhale carried across the air, reminding her that boundaries, once crossed, were hard to redraw.

Miles called out suddenly, waving at her to look. "Mom! It's staying up this time!"

She smiled, her chest tightening with a small rush of pride. "I see it, baby. That's perfect."

Anthone's voice came low, just enough for her to hear. "He's determined. Like you."

Vanessa looked straight ahead, pretending not to notice the edge in his compliment. "He's six," she said softly. "He's allowed to be."

Anthone chuckled, quiet and smooth. "Still. Determination starts young."

She turned to meet his eyes, or at least where his eyes should have been behind the lenses. "So does control."

For a moment, neither spoke. The wind shifted through the trees, scattering dry leaves over the mulch where Miles knelt, rebuilding again. His bridge leaned to one side, imperfect but steady. And for now, that was enough.

"You know," he said suddenly, his voice carrying easily across the few feet between them, "the Hawthorne Preparatory early decision deadline is coming up."

Vanessa didn't look at him right away. She lifted her coffee, took a slow sip, and only after setting the cup back down did she turn her head.

"First grade spots are competitive," Anthone continued, folding his arms a little tighter. His tone shifted into that familiar cadence, the one that always sounded like a closing argument. "They're molding leaders at five these days. Future surgeons don't play in the dirt all afternoon."

Vanessa drew in a quiet breath. She didn't flinch, and she didn't argue. That was their old pattern—his logic, her defense, a tug-of-war that always ended the same way: her tired, him unchanged.

"Miles is six," she said softly, her gaze moving toward her son. He was humming to himself, pressing a stick into the mulch with complete absorption. "He's building. That's enough for today."

The silence that followed felt heavier than the words had been.

Anthone shifted, pushing away from the fence to stand upright. "But if we start now—"

"We don't start anything," Vanessa said, her voice calm but edged with steel. She didn't raise it. She never needed to. The strength lay in her steadiness, in the quiet certainty that she would no longer be moved by his momentum.

Anthone's mouth twitched, as if he wanted to argue but thought better of it. Behind him, a child shrieked with laughter from the swings, and the sound broke the tension just enough for her to take another sip of coffee.

Miles glanced up and waved, proud of the new twig balanced across his miniature bridge. Vanessa smiled and waved back. The moment softened.

She didn't need to win this argument. She just

needed to hold the ground beneath her feet.

She turned fully toward him now, coffee still in hand. Her eyes met his over the rim of his sunglasses.

"I raise Miles. You visit."

The words dropped between them like stones into water, rippling the air. For a long moment, Anthone didn't move. Then his jaw tightened just enough for her to notice. His arms unfolded, hands slipping into his coat pockets—a gesture meant to seem effortless but heavy with bristling pride.

"You make it sound like I'm an outsider," he said finally.

"You are outside. You made that choice, when you asked if I'd consider other options." Her voice didn't rise, but the steadiness in it was its own kind of force. She let the phrase hang there, the old wound named but not reopened. "And I made mine—on solid ground. I raise a son who knows who he is. Not one raised to fear falling behind."

Anthone's jaw worked beneath the shadow of his sunglasses. He exhaled once, sharply, as though recalibrating something he couldn't quite fix. His hands left his pockets and came together in front of him, fingers lacing with quiet restraint.

"I'm just trying to give him advantages," he said.

The words were dressed in reason, polished and practiced, but Vanessa heard the undertone beneath— the same familiar chord he always played. To Anthone, advantage meant achievement. Childhood was an entry exam to adulthood. And joy, in his world, was only ever justified if it built a résumé.

She drew in a breath, steadying herself before answering. "And I'm giving him roots."

Miles called out just then, his voice bright and unbothered. "Mom! Look!"

He lifted a stick high in triumph, the fragile bridge beneath him wobbling but somehow still intact. His cheeks were flushed with pride, eyes seeking hers first—always hers. Vanessa smiled and raised her hand in return, the small gesture enough to make his grin stretch even wider.

Anthone glanced toward him but did not wave. His gaze slid back to Vanessa, unreadable behind the tinted glass.

J.P.Ellison

"You think love is enough?" he asked. His voice had softened, though it carried that familiar edge of disbelief. "The world doesn't care about roots. It doesn't hand out safety nets just because you cared enough."

Vanessa held her ground. "No. The world doesn't hand out safety nets. Which is exactly why I won't raise him to believe his worth is something he earns only by running faster than everyone else."

She lifted her coffee again, the lid warm against her lip though her throat felt dry. "He'll learn to climb, Anthone. But he won't climb a ladder you built only to pull it out from under him when he slips."

The words hung between them. Vanessa let the silence linger, unhurried and heavy. She had learned that not every pause needed filling. Some truths carried more strength when left to stand on their own.

"I'll keep you informed on his development," she said. "But if you can't show up without a blueprint and a brand strategy"—her eyes locked onto his, unrelenting—"don't show up at all."

The sentence landed. Final. Not a flare of anger

86

but a boundary laid in stone. Anthone's lips parted as if to argue, but no sound came. He looked away instead, chin angling toward the street where traffic slid past beyond the gates.

Miles laughed then, a bubbling sound that scattered across the backyard, untouched by the quiet storm only feet away. He crouched again, adding another twig.

Vanessa turned her gaze back to him, the tightness in her chest easing just slightly. When Miles's laughter rose again, she let it pull her focus. She stood, brushed crumbs from her coat, and walked toward the edge of the yard where her son knelt proudly over his uneven bridge.

"Pretty solid work," she said, crouching beside him.

Miles grinned, eyes glowing with that fierce kind of joy children carried when their creations held together against all odds. "It's strong, Mom. Wanna try walking on it?"

Vanessa chuckled softly, shaking her head. "Not today, engineer. My balance isn't what it used to be."

He nodded seriously and turned back to adjust a

stick, humming under his breath. Behind them, she heard the faint scrape of Anthone's shoes as he shifted his weight.

The distance between them wasn't measured in feet but in choices—his insistence on blueprints, her insistence on roots.

She straightened, watching Miles settle another twig into place. "Let's give it one more piece," she suggested. "Then we'll head inside for lunch."

"Peanut butter and bananas?" he asked, hopeful.

She smiled. "Always."

They packed up together—Miles carefully tucking the sturdier sticks into his backpack as if they were tools. Vanessa brushed mulch from his jacket. The small ordinariness of it filled her with more certainty than any lecture ever could.

As they left the backyard, Anthone walked a few steps behind. The sharpness had drained from his posture, leaving something else—defeat, maybe, or calculation. Vanessa didn't turn to read him. She didn't care enough to. All that mattered was the smile on Miles's face.

Sunlight glanced off the kitchen window as Vanessa rinsed dirt from their hands. Miles chattered through lunch—an endless stream about bridges, dinosaurs, and how peanut butter made him "strong like Hulk." Vanessa listened, letting the small moments stretch around her, anchoring her to something simple and true.

By Monday morning, the bananas were already browning. Vanessa turned one over in her hand, thumb brushing the softening peel, and sighed. A week ago, she had stretched the grocery budget by skipping the blueberries Miles loved, convincing herself bananas would last longer. They hadn't.

She dropped the spotted one into the freezer bag marked *smoothies someday*—her quiet ritual of refusing to waste—and set the last firm banana aside.

Miles clapped when he saw it, as though she had delivered a feast. The sound landed in her chest heavier than any tuition brochure. It was too much, sometimes, how small victories had to feel like triumphs. She forced a smile and poured his milk.

Love was enough, she reminded herself—but love

still cost $3.19 a bunch.

And for now, that was more than enough.

CHAPTER 11

Vanessa's Living Room, Late Evening

The lentil stew had been cleared, the bowls rinsed and stacked neatly in the sink, their earthy fragrance still lingering faintly in the air. Vanessa moved quietly as she placed the last spoon on the drying rack, the soft clink echoing in the cozy stillness of the house.

Upstairs, Miles slept soundly—a small shape bundled beneath his dinosaur-patterned quilt. One plastic stegosaurus was tucked firmly under his arm, as though the toy itself stood guard against bad dreams. The gentle rise and fall of his chest gave the house its heartbeat.

Downstairs, Vanessa was done for the night. She

curled up on the couch with her legs tucked beneath her, a mug of steaming herbal tea warming her palms. Across the room, Ethan stood before her bookshelf with exaggerated seriousness, head tilted, lips pursed, pretending to study which volume might contain the secret to life itself.

His fingers drifted along the spines—cookbooks, novels, a collection of essays she had promised herself she'd return to someday. He made a low humming noise, the sound he always used when performing deep thought.

"You know," he said casually, still facing the shelf, "if I moved in, your spice rack would finally reach its full potential."

The words landed with the kind of easy humor he carried into any space that felt too still. His tone was playful, yet beneath it hummed that familiar thread she recognized—the way Ethan often hid sincerity beneath the guise of teasing.

Vanessa raised an eyebrow, the corner of her mouth curving despite herself. "Oh?"

"I bring turmeric," he said with a solemn nod.

Then, after a beat, "And commitment."

The unexpected pairing cracked something open in her, and she laughed, the sound bubbling up before she could contain it. But the laughter caught halfway when he turned toward her. His usual thoughtful eyes had shifted, softened in a way that stripped the joke down to something raw.

"Look…" Ethan began. "Marriage—this FAR Act thing—it's only four years now." He stepped closer. "We can do four years, right?"

Before she could fully process the question, he dropped to one knee—not with a velvet box or a glittering ring, but with a grin stretched across his face. It was half-goofy, half-vulnerable. He extended his arms outward like a man taking a bow after a performance.

"Because I'm incredible," he declared, mock-grandiose. "Da da daaan! The best man on the planet. Besides Mr. Lewis, Mr. Brown, the Dean, Mr. Acorn… well, you know what I mean."

His ridiculousness earned another chuckle from her, though softer this time. Vanessa clutched her mug a little tighter, grounding herself in the warmth against her palms. She felt her lips pull into a smile, but it wavered.

Ethan noticed, of course. He always noticed.

"It could help," he added, his tone shifting again, this time more careful. He rose and settled onto the couch beside her, close enough that she could feel the heat of him even before his arm brushed the cushion. "With that student loan debt. I'm making close to two hundred grand now. And—" he tilted his head, offering a small smile, "I make a killer omelet."

"Ethan…" she said, her voice weighted with something more complicated than refusal, and more tangled than agreement.

"I know," he said gently, before she could continue. His grin softened into something fragile. "I do."

He leaned back against the couch, and for a moment the playfulness dissolved completely. His eyes searched hers.

"But I've been married before too."

He let the words linger in the space between them, a truth laid bare on the table.

"I wasn't loved," he continued, each word chosen with care. "I was expected. Expected to be everything. The man, the woman, the therapist, the coach, the income, the silence, the container."

The list landed heavily. Each word was a weight he had carried once, and still carried now.

Vanessa's chest tightened. She nodded slowly, her heart thudding against her ribs, because she understood. She understood more than she wished she did.

"And you?" Ethan asked softly after a pause, his voice like a hand extended into the dark.

Vanessa drew in a breath, her fingers trembling slightly around her mug. Meeting his gaze felt like peeling back layers she had pressed down for years.

"I was an anchor," she said finally, her voice so quiet she wondered if he truly heard. "An anchor in someone else's storm. And when I needed saving, I was called selfish for drowning."

The words escaped with a raw ache. For a heartbeat, the room seemed to inhale with her.

Ethan didn't speak right away. He simply reached

for her hand, his touch careful, patient. His fingers closed around hers, warm and steady.

"I'm not asking for vows," he said. "I'm asking for us. In whatever form makes you feel like you're still you."

Her throat tightened. "Even if it's not marriage?"

His lips curved into the smallest, most genuine of smiles. "Especially if it's not marriage."

Vanessa studied him. Her tea had gone lukewarm, untouched in her other hand. Her heart sat somewhere between the scars of her past and the soft outline of something new. She swallowed, then asked the question that trembled on the edge of hope.

"And if it is?"

The words hung in the air like incense smoke— fragile, persistent, impossible to wave away.

Ethan didn't answer right away. He let the silence stretch, the kind that spoke of care rather than hesitation. His thumb moved slowly along the side of her palm, a small, steady gesture that held her in the present while the rest of her threatened to drift.

Vanessa waited. The weight of her own question

pressed like a stone against her ribs. She wanted to take it back—to hide it somewhere safe inside her caution—but she couldn't. It had escaped, born from that stubborn, unkillable seed of hope that still lived in her despite everything.

"And if it is?" she asked again, softer this time, daring him to tell her that marriage, to him, was still just a joke told over turmeric and omelets.

Ethan exhaled slowly, and for the first time that night, he looked less like the man who joked his way through tenderness and more like someone standing unguarded. His smile didn't disappear; it softened into something smaller, sadder, yet steadier.

"If it is," he said, almost a whisper, "then it has to be different from what either of us had before."

Her heart stumbled. "Different how?"

"Not cages," he said quietly. "Not a life built on pretending. No more swallowing the truth just to keep the peace. No more performing strength so the other person doesn't have to see where we're breaking." He turned his palm upward, brushing his fingers against hers. "It would mean saying the things we're afraid of.

Even when it's messy. Even when it doesn't make sense yet."

Vanessa swallowed hard, her throat tight. Those were the words she had needed to hear years ago. She thought of the nights she cried quietly into her pillow, afraid to wake the boy sleeping down the hall, and the mornings she painted on a smile so carefully that even she started to believe it. For the first time, she wondered what it might feel like to be seen before she had to hide.

"You make it sound easy," she whispered.

Ethan gave a low, rueful chuckle. "God, no. I make omelets easy. This? This is terrifying."

That earned him a flicker of a smile, small but real, even as her eyes glistened with something she refused to let fall. The sound of a distant car hummed past the open window, the quiet settling again like dust between them.

"You'd really... what? Sign yourself up for four years of a binding contract just to—what—prove a point?" she asked, though her voice lacked its usual defense.

"I'd sign myself up," Ethan said, leaning closer. His elbows rested on his knees, voice softening. "Because I want mornings with you. Because I want Miles' dinosaur on the coffee table next to my coffee mug. Because—"

He stopped, breath catching. The emotion tightened his throat, the confession crowding his chest until he tried to break it with humor. "Because turmeric. Obviously."

Vanessa pressed her lips together, trying not to laugh, but it came out anyway—thin, trembling at the edges. What began as amusement slipped into something else, something tender and raw that made her chest ache.

"Don't," she whispered.

Ethan blinked. "Don't what?"

"Don't joke your way out of this." The plea in her voice startled even her. It wasn't accusation. It was fear—of believing too much.

Ethan's eyes softened again, the grin fading, replaced by a steadiness that pulled her in before she could look away. "I'm not," he said quietly. "Not this time."

The air shifted. Neither moved, caught in the fragile space between what had been said and what could no longer be taken back. Vanessa's fingers tightened around her cup, the warmth seeping through cardboard into her palms.

Outside, Miles' laughter rang out, bright and distant, a sound that broke through the moment like sunlight cutting fog. Ethan glanced toward the window, then back at her, his expression unreadable but open in a way she hadn't seen before.

Vanessa inhaled slowly, her heartbeat too loud in her ears. There was something terrifying in how much she wanted to believe him—how much she already did.

The room grew very silent. The only sounds were the steady tick of the kitchen clock, the low hum of the refrigerator, and the faint shifting of pipes behind the walls. Time itself seemed to hold its breath.

Vanessa felt every beat of her pulse in her palm beneath the light brush of his thumb. The simple touch was grounding and dangerous all at once. She wanted to believe him—wanted it so fiercely it frightened her. She had believed before, and it had nearly broken her.

"Ethan…" She started, then faltered. Her eyes dropped to the mug cooling in her other hand. The steam had vanished, but she clutched it as though warmth might return if she only held on tightly enough. "I don't know if I can risk… another collapse."

He tilted his head, studying her with the quiet patience that came when words mattered. "You don't have to. Not all at once. Not tonight. Hell, not even next month." His thumb brushed her hand again, a small promise in the motion. "But you asked if it is." He paused, drew in a steadying breath, and when he spoke again, his voice had deepened. "If it is, then it's because we both decide every damn day that we still want it. Not because some law says we have to."

Her lips parted, the question barely a whisper. "Every day?"

"Every day," he repeated, nodding once. "And if the answer's ever no—then we say it. We don't have to pretend, or drag each other through years of storms out of pride. We step back before we drown."

For a long moment, neither moved. The clock ticked on, marking seconds that felt heavier than hours. Vanessa stared at him, trying to tell where courage ended and foolish hope began

Vanessa closed her eyes, a faint shiver moving through her. His words pressed straight into the bruise she still carried, the one that had never fully faded. When she opened her eyes again, Ethan was still watching her—not with demand, but with patience. That patience was the most dangerous thing of all. It made her want to believe.

She sat very still, his words circling inside her like stones dropped into water, rippling outward into places she tried not to look.

"You talk about stepping back before we drown," she said at last, her voice brittle, "but when you're already under, they just call you weak for not knowing how to swim."

Ethan's brow furrowed, his hand tightening gently around hers. "Is that what he called you?"

Her lips pressed together. She didn't answer right

away. The truth sat in her throat, jagged and heavy. When she finally spoke, it came out sideways, softened by weariness. "I think... he believed I was supposed to hold everything together. The bills. His moods. My job. Miles. Myself. And when I couldn't... when I asked for help..." She shook her head, the memory pushing against her ribs like something alive. "He told me I was selfish for not being stronger."

Ethan didn't move, didn't speak. He just let her say it. Somehow, that was worse—because it meant he was really listening.

The silence stretched until she forced herself to meet his eyes. They weren't filled with pity, which she had feared. Instead, they were steady, carrying a sadness that seemed to belong to both of them.

The air between them thickened, not with tension, but with recognition—the quiet acknowledgment of two people who understood what it meant to break and still reach for something whole.

"You were drowning," he said quietly. "And he called it selfish."

Her throat tightened. "Yes."

Ethan's jaw clenched. For a moment, he looked like he wanted to spit fire on behalf of the woman beside him, but instead he exhaled slowly, the fight settling into the space behind his eyes. His thumb traced another small circle against her palm, patient and steady.

"That's not selfish," he said finally. "That's human."

Vanessa's breath caught. A small, unexpected warmth spread through her chest, warring with the ache that had lived there too long.

"Don't make it sound so simple," she said, her voice breaking. "Because it wasn't. It isn't. I had a son to think about. I still do."

At that, Ethan leaned back slightly, nodding. He glanced toward the ceiling, toward the quiet above them where Miles slept with his dinosaur tucked tight against his chest. The image softened his features.

"I know," he said. "And I don't want to take that lightly." He hesitated, choosing his words with care. "You've both been through storms. I'm not here to erase them or pretend I can. I just… I want to stand in them with you."

Vanessa's eyes flickered, caught between disbelief and the fragile pull of hope. "Do you know what that really means?" she asked, the words trembling as they escaped.

"I think so." He gave a small shrug, an attempt to fold sincerity into humor again, though his tone couldn't quite disguise the weight of what he felt. "It means stepping on Legos at three in the morning. It means dinosaur trivia quizzes at breakfast. It means not being jealous when you and Miles gang up on me during family movie night."

She tried to hold back the smile tugging at her lips, but it slipped through anyway, faint and real. For the first time that night, the air felt less like it was closing in and more like it might open.

Vanessa let out a small, strangled laugh, but the tears slid down her cheeks anyway.

"And it means," Ethan continued more quietly, "that I don't just marry you, if that's what this is. I'll marry him too. And if he never calls me dad, if he only ever sees me as the guy who makes omelets and loses at Uno—that's enough."

The tears came faster now. She tried to wipe them away with the back of her hand, but Ethan beat her to it, brushing lightly at her cheek with his thumb. The gesture was so gentle it undid her.

"I don't know if I can trust that," she whispered.

"I know," he said simply.

The two of them sat there, side by side, the distance between laughter and tears narrowing into something raw. The tea had gone cold completely, but Vanessa still held the mug as if afraid to set it down and lose her anchor. Ethan leaned back slightly, giving her the room she didn't ask for but needed, his hand still tangled with hers.

His voice, when he spoke next, was softer, almost tentative. "You don't have to trust it yet. Just... don't shut it out."

Vanessa set her mug down at last. It landed with a muted thud on the side table, forgotten steam long since fled. Her palms felt strangely bare without it. She flexed her fingers once, unsure whether to hold on or to let go.

For a moment she imagined another life—mornings filled with turmeric and laughter, with Miles proudly correcting Ethan's dinosaur facts, with warmth that didn't feel like duty but like air. The image came so vividly it ached, pressing against the edges of her heart like something half-remembered.

Ethan watched her in the quiet, not asking for anything more than the space to stay. And in that silence, fragile but whole, something in her steadied—not trust, not yet, but the faint outline of where it might begin.

"What if I ruin it?" she asked suddenly. The words slipped out before she could stop them.

Ethan blinked, startled. "Ruin it?"

"Yes." She pulled her hand from his and wrapped her arms around herself as if she could keep the fear contained that way. "What if I don't know how to love right anymore? What if I hold on too tight, or not enough? What if…" Her breath trembled. "What if the storm comes back, and I can't keep anyone afloat?"

Ethan didn't interrupt. He didn't laugh it off or tell her she was being dramatic. He let the questions hang there, heavy as fog, letting them fill the space between them until her voice faded. Then he leaned forward, resting his forearms on his knees, his gaze steady on hers.

"Then we learn how to swim together."

She let out a sound that broke halfway between a scoff and a sob. "That's not an answer."

"It's the only one I've got," he said. "Because I don't know what the storms will look like. But I know I'd rather be in them with you than safe somewhere else without you."

Vanessa turned to him then—really turned. Her eyes searched his face for cracks, for anything rehearsed or false, anything that might let her retreat before she fell any further. But all she found was the same steady, infuriating patience, the quiet belief that she wasn't as broken as she thought.

Something inside her shifted, slow and fragile, like a door unlatched for the first time in years.

The room felt smaller suddenly. She realized with a jolt that his knee brushed hers, that the heat of him seeped through the narrow space between them. Yet, even with the warmth of everything pressing in, she didn't pull away. Maybe this was a sign she was more ready than she thought.

Vanessa's mind drifted, as it often did in the quiet after a storm. Memories of that night with Ethan slipped in uninvited—the way his hands had found hers, the weight and warmth of his body close, the soft laughter that had followed every whispered word. The thought lingered like a low hum beneath her ribs, leaving behind a flutter that surprised her in the middle of her day. It wasn't just desire. It was the deep calm of being seen—truly seen—in a way no one else ever had.

A small shiver ran through her at the memory of his smile. She shook her head, half-laughing at herself, but the sound was tender, not scolding. Weeks later, the recollection still settled somewhere between restlessness and peace.

She closed her eyes for a moment, letting that feeling stretch quietly through her—like sunlight after rain. The warmth wasn't fleeting; it was something that had stayed, even when she wasn't looking. A reminder that connection didn't have to mean collapse, that love could hold both safety and fire.

And for the first time in a long while, Vanessa let herself believe she might be brave enough to feel it again.

CHAPTER 12

Evening Phone Calls

Vanessa stood by the kitchen sink, one hand cradling her phone, the other wrapped around a half-full glass of water. The rim was cool beneath her fingers, condensation tracing slow, uncertain paths across her knuckles. She hadn't realized how tightly she was holding it until a dull ache pulsed through her wrist, tendons taut with the strain. The edge of the counter pressed into her hip, grounding her in the small circle of light spilling from the overhead lamp—a reminder that she was still here, in this quiet room, even as her mind drifted somewhere else entirely.

The dishwasher hummed softly at her side, a low

mechanical rhythm that should have been calming. Every so often, a faint clink of plates broke through, the metallic notes swallowed quickly by the steady rush of water. It was an ordinary sound, the kind that usually slipped into the background of evenings like this. But tonight, it grated against her nerves. The house carried its usual rhythm, steady and sure, while her body moved to a pulse she couldn't quiet.

A faint lemon scent filled the air, the detergent mixing with the warmth of steam rising from the dishwasher. The smell was sharp, almost sterile, clinging to the damp edges of the room. Beyond the window above the sink, darkness pressed against the glass, her reflection staring back at her—a faint, tired silhouette caught in the faint shimmer of kitchen light. Her hair framed her face in soft disarray, a few damp strands clinging to her cheek.

For a long moment, she simply stood there, the phone resting loosely in her hand. The silence between each heartbeat felt heavier than the sound of the machine beside her. It wasn't just an evening phone call she was waiting for—it was the weight of something unspoken, something that had followed her into this quiet hour.

Upstairs, Miles was asleep. She had checked twice already, though once would have been enough. Both times, she had moved softly up the narrow staircase, careful where she placed her feet on the worn steps. The old wood always protested, a gentle creak that seemed too loud in the stillness.

The first time, she lingered outside his door, listening for the faint rhythm of his breathing, the subtle rise and fall that told her he was deep in dreams. The second time, she cracked the door just enough to see him sprawled across tangled sheets, one arm curled around his stuffed dinosaur, his mouth slightly open. The sight of him, small and unguarded, should have centered her. It usually did. But tonight it only made the restlessness in her chest feel sharper, more alive.

He was safe. The house was safe. She repeated it to herself like a mantra, yet the safety felt too tight, pressing in around her until she could hardly breathe. The silence of the rooms below carried a strange weight, heavy and still, as if her thoughts could echo there unchecked. And in that quiet, Anthone's voice returned.

It lingered in the air, threaded through the walls, impossible to shut out. She could almost hear him still—the faint scuff of his shoes across the hardwood, the deliberate rhythm of his movements, the arrogance hidden inside his easy posture. He always leaned against the counter like he owned the space, his eyes gliding over everything as though taking inventory.

It had started, as it always did, with something small. The dishes. Maybe she had left a few plates by the sink after dinner, telling herself she'd get to them later.

"You know kids learn habits from what they see, not what they're told," he had said.

He hadn't looked at her when he spoke, just at the plates, his voice wrapped in that polite restraint that sounded like care to anyone who didn't know better. Her throat had tightened then, muscles drawing taut in defense.

The instinct to answer back rose hard in her chest—to tell him that sometimes dishes waited because bedtime stories came first, that a messy sink wasn't a reflection of her worth. But she had swallowed it. The words caught behind her teeth, small and rough, until silence became the only thing she could manage.

He thrived on that—on pushing just far enough to wound, never far enough to be caught. It wasn't cruelty in the way most people imagined. Every comment arrived dressed as concern, every observation polished until it gleamed like advice. But beneath that polish was judgment, and beneath judgment was control.

He wielded both with quiet precision, shaping the air around him until a room bent to his presence. Even when he left, it never felt like an absence. It felt like residue, a film she couldn't scrub away. His shadow seemed to linger in the corners, his voice caught in the walls. The air held his temperature long after the door had closed.

Vanessa pressed her thumb to the glass, dragging a faint line through the condensation as if she could erase him. The motion left a clear streak, her reflection divided by that small act of defiance. Her stomach tightened. The silence around her pressed closer, thick and unrelenting. She needed to tell someone before it swallowed her whole.

She picked up the phone and dialed.

"He's doing it again," she said, skipping any greeting.

The sharpness in her voice startled her. It came out rough, alive with anger she hadn't realized she still carried. It didn't sound like her—it sounded like someone braver, someone less tired.

There was no hesitation on the other end. She knew Ethan had answered by the faint rustle of movement, fabric brushing against fabric, the small sound of him drawing breath before the quiet stretched out again. He didn't rush to fill it. Ethan never rushed. That, more than anything, was why she had called him and no one else. He let silence stand without trying to erase it.

"Anthone," she said, her voice lower now. "He came to 'visit,' but it felt more like a performance review."

"He's got opinions about everything," she went on, the words spilling faster now, as though once opened they refused to stop. "Miles's shoes are too worn, apparently. He says the playground nearby is too small, that the bigger one across town would build more 'resilience.' He talks about schools, extracurriculars, what will look good on some imagined résumé years from now. Even how I should think about the 'long game.'"

The long game. The phrase echoed in her head, heavy and rehearsed. She'd heard him say it countless times, always with that same measured patience, that gentle tone people mistook for wisdom. To her, it had always sounded like correction—like a teacher reminding a child to sit up straight.

Her mind replayed the scene from earlier, the kitchen lit in its soft evening glow. Anthone had leaned back against the counter, hands in his pockets, surveying everything around him as if the room were a stage and she'd forgotten her lines. His expression had been almost pleasant, the kind of calm that carried its own quiet authority.

His eyes had traveled over the magnets on the fridge, the pile of unopened mail, the scuffed sneakers by the back door. None of it should have mattered. None of it said anything about her. But under his gaze, each detail seemed to transform—into proof, into judgment, into the shape of something she couldn't defend. Evidence of neglect. Evidence of failure. Evidence that she wasn't enough.

Her fingers tightened around the glass, the rim pressing cold and firm into her skin until it hurt. In her mind, she could still see him standing there, inhabiting her kitchen like it belonged to him, like she was the one visiting.

On the other end of the line, Ethan said nothing. He didn't ask for context or offer sympathy. He didn't fill the silence with words meant to comfort. He just stayed there, steady and quiet, his breathing the only proof she wasn't alone.

She closed her eyes briefly, the glass trembling slightly in her hand. "It's a visitation, Ethan," she added. "Not a goddamn examination."

The words were sharp, honed by the frustration she had held back until now. Her pulse throbbed against her throat, a dull hammering that echoed behind her jaw. Her other hand tapped the side of the glass once, twice, then went still, as if the motion could quiet the tension coiling inside her.

Finally, Ethan's voice came through, steady and calm, like a current moving just beneath the surface.

"Yeah," he said. "That's a line. And he keeps trying to blur it."

Vanessa exhaled, though it came out more like a shudder than a breath. She lifted the glass to her lips but didn't drink. The cool, metallic rim rested against her mouth, grounding her. It wasn't about thirst; it was about having a barrier, something tangible to hold between herself and the silence that otherwise threatened to swallow her whole.

Time stretched, slow and deliberate. And yet, even in that quiet, she didn't feel alone. Ethan's presence had a weight that didn't demand words. He didn't calculate a response or try to fix anything. He simply existed in the space beside her, steady and unwavering. It was strange, and rare, to feel seen like that—to have someone hear without rushing, without judgment.

She swallowed against the cool edge of the glass,

her voice softening, slipping out almost against her own will. "He doesn't even see Miles," she whispered, her throat catching halfway through the sentence. "He sees a résumé in progress. A legacy to polish."

The bitterness in her voice surprised her, but she hadn't softened it. Each word dripped with acid, deliberate and sharp.

"And you?" Ethan asked gently.

"He sees me as a mistake that turned into a responsibility," Vanessa whispered, her words trembling on the edge of the line.

"Then he's not looking hard enough," Ethan said. His tone was low, almost matter-of-fact, but warmth threaded through it, softening the bluntness. "Because what I see? You made a life. You're raising a whole person—with depth, joy, imagination. That's not a résumé. That's a miracle you live with every single day."

Vanessa closed her eyes. The words landed differently than advice, differently than comfort. Advice always carried a faint implication: you're doing it wrong, you need to fix it. Comfort often tried to wrap a gauze around the pain, to cover it, to hush it.

Ethan's words did neither. They met the wound directly, acknowledged her anger without flinching, and then quietly reminded her of the life she had built— the truth beneath everything else that had been overlooked.

She trusted him for that reason. Not because he said the right thing, but because he never said it to fix her. He said it to remind her of what was already true—what she sometimes forgot when Anthone's voice grew too loud in her head.

"Sometimes I feel like I still have to prove something to him," she admitted, her words small, almost ashamed, as if confessing something illicit.

"You don't," Ethan said softly. "You already did the hard part—you set a boundary. Now you're just holding it. That's not weakness, V. That's maintenance. That's strength."

She let out a slow breath. "Thanks," she said, her voice stripped of the earlier bite. "I don't need a fixer."

"Good," Ethan replied. There was the faintest warmth in his tone, like a candle lit in a dark room. "Because I'd rather be your witness."

Vanessa's chest tightened—not painfully, but with a fullness she hadn't expected. A pause lingered, then a small laugh slipped from her, light and real. "That was kind of corny."

"True," Ethan said, without missing a beat. She could hear the shrug in his voice. "But also sincere. That's the only currency I trade in."

She smiled despite herself, warmth blooming quietly in her chest. "Want to come by tomorrow?" she asked, a note of hope threading through her words. "I'm making lentil stew. Miles asked if you could bring the dinosaur book again."

"Wouldn't miss it."

CHAPTER 13

Vows

They didn't send invitations. There were no cream-colored envelopes, no meticulously embossed stationery, no curling calligraphy announcing a day to be remembered. No list of names checked twice, no painstaking hours spent deciding who should sit beside whom, no anxious deliberations over tablecloths or chair colors. There was no band, no first dance, no last song to mark the hours. There was only the day itself—quiet, unassuming, and perfectly theirs.

It was a late autumn afternoon, the kind that carried a crispness that kissed bare skin without biting, the kind where the sky hovered in muted grays and silvers as though to soften the light just for them. Wind moved steadily through the trees, tugging at branches, rattling the few stubborn leaves clinging to them. Fallen leaves spiraled along the garden path, crunching softly underfoot like whispers of seasons past.

Around twenty people had gathered in the garden behind a friend's farmhouse, drawn not by ceremony but by the gentle intimacy of it. Some clutched mugs of steaming cider, their fingers warming against the chill; others tucked hands into coats or shawls, leaning into each other as they waited. Voices rose and fell in murmured conversation, drifting with the breeze. A distant bark broke the quiet for a moment, then faded again. No one needed a schedule or a master of ceremonies. Everyone simply knew why they were there.

Vanessa stood beneath a canopy of golden leaves, each one catching the afternoon light like tiny lanterns. Her dress was unadorned, soft fabric that moved with the wind, brushing against her legs as if in quiet approval. It was not a dress meant to impress anyone; it was a dress that was simply hers. Her hair caught hints of sunlight in its strands, and when she smiled, it was as though the garden itself leaned closer to share the moment.

Around her, friends lingered in gentle clusters. Some laughed quietly over shared memories; others watched in stillness, aware that the space between heartbeats seemed stretched, meaningful. A few children ran ahead along the garden path, leaves flying up around their shoes in tiny whirlwinds, their laughter threading through the autumn air. Every sound, every movement, seemed to underscore the simplicity of the day. This was a vow not announced with grandeur but held in quiet presence, in the way a wind-chilled hand fit perfectly in another, in the way sunlight brushed across gold and amber, in the way the heart recognized itself in another without need for words.

And there they were—together, in that understated perfection, ready to promise each other everything without fanfare.

The sleeves of her dress brushed against her wrists, and when she clasped her hands in front of her, there was no tremor. Her hands were steady—warm, solid, grounded in a calm certainty.

Miles stood a little distance away, clutching a bouquet almost comically large for his small frame. A jumble of wildflowers and late-season blooms—sunflowers, chrysanthemums, sprigs of lavender—was tied together with a simple loop of twine. He grinned with unselfconscious delight, wide and gap-toothed, the missing front tooth giving his smile a charm all its own. He shifted from foot to foot, as though standing still for this long were its own quiet trial, yet his eyes sparkled with excitement. Every now and then, he stole a glance at his mother, then quickly back at Ethan, as if checking that the world was still right where it belonged.

Ethan stood across from her. His jacket, slightly too formal for him, hung on his frame in contrast to the worn sweaters and rolled-up sleeves she knew so well. She suspected he'd never wear it again after this day—but the jacket didn't matter. Nothing could compete with the way his eyes held hers, unwavering, unblinking, as if the rest of the world had been folded away. Every other sight, every other sound, seemed irrelevant in the face of that gaze.

She drew in a steady breath, feeling the weight of the moment settle around her like the soft autumn light. Then she spoke, her voice calm but carrying the kind of clarity that made the quiet air seem to listen.

"I used to think love had to look a certain way."

Her words floated in the space between them, honest and unadorned. "Big gestures. Perfect timing. Picture-worthy moments."

A pause, brief but deliberate, allowed the memory of those old expectations to drift between them. Her lips curved faintly—not into a smile, but in recognition of the truth she had once chased. "And for a while, I lived like that. Performing, proving, posing. Hoping someone would see me—and stay."

The words hung between them, fragile and full, suspended in the quiet garden. A soft rustle of leaves whispered through the air, carrying the faint scent of late autumn. She glanced at Ethan, the memory of all those years surfacing briefly—the years she had measured herself against impossible standards, molded herself into shapes that weren't her own. Her gaze lingered on him, and in that silence, it seemed to say, *you saw me anyway.*

"But you," she continued, her voice softening, carrying a gentleness that made the space between them feel sacred. "You didn't fall in love with the version of me I'd rehearsed. You stayed for the silence." She let the words hover, giving them weight. "For the mess. For the mornings I couldn't speak, and the nights I couldn't sleep."

Her throat tightened with gratitude, a warm ache that made her pause. Her voice softened, quiet yet unwavering, a truth that didn't need to be loud to be felt. "I don't vow to always know what I'm doing," she said, a corner of her mouth lifting in something that was half-smile, half-acknowledgment of her own imperfections. "I don't vow to never feel afraid. Because I will. I know I will."

A breeze stirred, brushing a strand of hair across her cheek. She didn't move it aside, letting it rest there, a simple proof of life's quiet interruptions. "But I vow to stay. Present. Honest. Open. Not because love is easy, but because it's worth showing up for."

The words seemed to linger longer than the wind, filling the space around them with a kind of quiet reverence. Each one was a promise carved in the simplicity of being together, in the acknowledgment of flaws, in the bravery of vulnerability. Around them, the garden held its breath, the golden leaves catching the light as if leaning closer to witness the moment, the heart of their vows made visible in the soft, autumnal glow.

Her lips curved at last, a true smile finding its place. "I'm not starting over," she said softly. "I'm beginning well."

The phrase lingered in the air, like the final note of a song that needed no applause. Around them, the guests remained quiet, hushed by the honesty of it— the way truth can still a room more completely than ceremony ever could.

Ethan stepped forward, closing the small distance between them until only the rhythm of their joined breath filled the space. He took both her hands in his, thumbs brushing lightly over the backs of her knuckles—a touch both grounding and reverent.

His eyes never left hers. "I don't need to rescue you," he said, voice steady, carrying certainty. "And you've never asked me to."

"What we have," he continued, his words unfolding naturally now, "isn't about fixing what's broken. It's about building something beautiful with what's still strong."

He let the thought hang between them, letting its weight sink in, then softened his gaze. "And there's so much strength here, V. In you. In Miles. In us. Enough to carry us through more than either of us could alone."

He smiled then—the kind of smile that reached his eyes and stayed there. "I vow to walk with you," he said, each word deliberate. "To speak when it matters. To listen when silence is louder than words. To stay soft in the hard seasons. And to laugh at Miles' dinosaur impressions, even when they make no sense."

A breeze stirred, tugging lightly at the hem of her dress and tousling his hair, as if the world itself leaned closer to witness the promises between them.

The guests chuckled softly, a warm, unforced

sound that broke through like sunlight filtering through branches. Miles grinned wide, clearly proud to be named in Ethan's vow, holding his oversized bouquet a little higher as if he'd been singled out for honor.

"I vow to show up. On the sunny days, and the stormy ones. Not with perfection, but with presence," Ethan said, his voice quieter now, intimate, almost confiding.

When he finished, silence stretched again—not the uneasy kind, but the kind that carries weight, the hush of leaves shifting overhead, of wind moving gently through open space, of people holding something fragile between them and unwilling to disturb it. Vanessa's eyes stayed locked on Ethan's face. The warmth in his tone pressed against her chest, settling into the space where fear had once lived. Her throat tightened—not with doubt, but with the sudden, undeniable weight of being seen so completely.

There was no thunderous applause, no cueing music, no clapping to push the moment forward. Just the soft rustle of branches, the faint shuffle of someone shifting in the grass, the quiet acknowledgement of a truth laid bare.

Around them, guests leaned in subtly, almost unconsciously, drawn closer by the gravity of the words and the delicate sincerity that hung in the crisp autumn air. Every inhale, every pause, felt sacred, as if the world itself had held its breath to give their vows space to settle, unhurried and whole.

One woman dabbed at her cheek with the edge of her sleeve. Another clasped her partner's hand, fingers tightening in a quiet, shared recognition of something timeless. But the couple at the center hardly noticed. Vanessa breathed in slowly, grounding herself in the moment, while Ethan's hands tightened around hers— just a fraction—not to claim her, but to say simply: *I'm here.*

The wind carried the faint smell of freshly baked bread again, now mingled with the smoky scent of a fire burning inside the farmhouse to ward off the evening chill. The mingling scents felt like a promise of their own—warmth and sustenance waiting just beyond the vows, a gentle reminder that life went on in ordinary magic even as extraordinary moments unfolded.

Ethan's eyes softened as he looked at her, and then he smiled—a smile that said he wasn't rushing past this moment, wasn't eager to move on to what came next. He was here, fully present. His words replayed themselves in Vanessa's mind like echoes: *I vow to walk with you. To speak when needed. To listen more.*

She thought of the nights when silence had weighed heavier than words, when exhaustion had pressed against her bones like a second skin, and how Ethan had sat there anyway, offering nothing more than his presence. She thought of Miles—the way Ethan crouched to his level, patient and unhurried, treating him as a whole person, not an accessory to her life. She remembered the dinosaur impressions that made no sense but drew laughter until tears stung their eyes. And that vow to laugh, even in the midst of absurdity—it wasn't frivolous. It was devotion in disguise, a promise embedded in every shared smile, every patient gesture, every echo of presence over time.

The moment stretched, gentle and infinite, held in the hush of leaves, in the warmth of a fire unseen, in the quiet acknowledgment of a family that had already begun in laughter, honesty, and unwavering love.

The guests lingered in quiet smiles, exchanging subtle glances as if they, too, had been let in on the truth: that love was not built on spectacle or perfection, but on presence, on showing up for one another day after day, in both the ordinary and the extraordinary.

"And most of all…" Ethan's final words echoed in Vanessa's mind, soft and deliberate.

Vanessa's eyes glimmered again, but this time it wasn't from nerves or even gratitude. It was recognition—a deep, steady awareness that she was not, and never would be, alone. Not as long as he stood beside her, his hands holding hers with quiet certainty, his eyes anchoring her heart.

They kissed then, not with urgency or grandeur, but with a steadiness that made the world seem to pause. It was less like fireworks and more like breath— consistent, reliable, and entirely enough. His hands lingered on hers, reluctant to release, even as their lips parted, and the memory of that touch promised constancy long after the moment had passed.

In the distance, the farmhouse glowed warmly. Later, when string lights flickered overhead and soup steamed in wide bowls, bread broken and passed around, there would be laughter and stories. Miles would raise his small glass of apple juice, grinning so wide it seemed to stretch across his entire face. He would make a toast in words half-muddled but overflowing with intent, and the sound of it would ripple through the gathering like sunlight breaking through clouds, warm and uncontainable.

But not yet. Not now.

For now, Vanessa and Ethan stood together, hand in hand, letting the fading light of late afternoon drape around them like a gentle cloak. The last gold of the leaves above glowed in the slanting sun, painting the garden in a warmth that seemed almost reverent. Even the wind held itself, stirring only softly, as if to allow the moment to linger a heartbeat longer.

They weren't starting over. They weren't stepping into a clean slate. They were beginning well—anchored in truth, in devotion, and in the quiet joy of simply being together. And in that simple, profound beginning, the world seemed to hold its breath alongside them, giving space for love to settle, patient and unhurried, into the life they were building.

CHAPTER 14

The Trigger

The morning light fell in gentle stripes across the kitchen floor, filtering through the slats of the half-open blinds. Dust motes floated lazily in the warm beams, catching the sun like tiny sparks. Steam curled from a mug on the counter, carrying the faint scent of cinnamon and something citrusy—maybe a hint of orange peel from the tea Ethan had brewed for Vanessa.

Miles was sprawled on the floor near the window, surrounded by a small universe of toys—dinosaurs frozen mid-roar, wooden cars lined up as if ready to race, and a spaceship missing one fin. His quiet sound effects punctuated the hush of the house, a soft punctuation to the slow rhythm of morning. Occasionally, he tapped the finless ship against the floor, as if testing its aerodynamics, then made a triumphant little squeak.

Vanessa stood at the sink, rinsing a plate that didn't really need rinsing. Her fingers moved automatically beneath the stream of warm water, tracing the familiar shape of the ceramic, while her mind drifted elsewhere. She was tangled in the slow rhythm of this new life, feeling its weight and its promise all at once. The house still smelled faintly of paint and pine from the shelves Ethan had built last weekend, and she could hear the faint creak of the floorboards settling beneath her bare feet. Framed photos sat half-arranged on the table, snapshots of laughter and quiet moments, reminders that they were inching closer to feeling like this place could truly be home.

Ethan sat at the breakfast table behind her, one hand curled around his coffee mug, the other holding a folded section of the newspaper. He wasn't reading aloud, but she could tell by the furrow in his brow that something in the headlines had caught him. There was a shadow of tension in the set of his shoulders, subtle but enough for Vanessa to notice without turning. For a moment, she wondered if she should ask, or if some things were better left unspoken over breakfast.

"Mama, look!" Miles' voice cut through the quiet, bright and unguarded, pulling her out of her reverie. He held up a small plastic figure with triumphant pride. "He's flying now."

Vanessa leaned over slightly, her hands still wet from the rinse, and smiled. "He sure is," she said softly, feeling the warmth of the sunlight and the faint, comforting scent of cinnamon wrap around her like a hug. She glanced at Ethan, whose eyes had softened despite the crease in his brow, and for a fleeting moment, the tension in the room seemed to melt, leaving behind only the small, perfect world of a morning just waking.

She turned, her voice automatically warm. "He looks fast."

"He's saving the city," Miles said matter-of-factly, returning to his play, the tiny feet of his dinosaurs clattering softly against the floor.

Ethan's chair creaked as he shifted. The sound drew her eyes to him—not just because of the motion, but because of the pause that followed, heavy and deliberate. The faint scent of coffee lingered around him, grounding the moment in quiet domesticity, yet somehow it did little to ease the tension she suddenly felt coiling in her stomach.

She wiped her hands on a towel, the cloth rough and familiar beneath her fingers. "What?"

He looked up, eyes darkened with something she couldn't name. "You don't want to start your day with this."

Her stomach tightened, though she didn't yet know why. "With what?"

He hesitated, as if weighing how much to reveal, then unfolded the newspaper and laid it flat on the table. The headline stretched across the top, bold and declarative, demanding attention:

"RESTORE BUILDING BRIDGES ACT CLEARS FINAL. REVIEW—RETROACTIVE MARITAL REVISIONS BEGIN NEXT WEEK."

The words didn't register at first. They were a string

of bureaucratic language, precise and sterile, almost harmless in their officialness, the way government statements often were. But something about the phrasing—*retroactive marital revisions*—pricked at her like an unexpected chill, tugging at the edges of a memory she hadn't realized was still so sensitive.

"What does that mean?" she asked quietly, her voice catching just slightly.

Ethan scanned the smaller print, his finger tracing the columns like a guide through the unfamiliar terrain. "It says the act will allow tribunals—both civil and ecclesiastical—to review past annulments filed under certain emotional grounds. They're calling it a move toward 'ethical consistency.'"

He looked up at her, his expression carefully neutral, but she could see the hint of concern lurking there, behind the measured calm. Vanessa felt a flutter of unease, a whisper in the pit of her stomach that she tried to ignore. Miles' laughter rang out in the background as he sent a spaceship tumbling across the floor, blissfully unaware of the storm of words that had just entered their morning.

Vanessa's chest tightened. "Emotional grounds?"

He nodded slowly, eyes steady but soft. "Like 'irreconcilable differences.' Or 'incompatibility.'"

The towel slipped from her hand, landing soundlessly on the counter. It was a small, inconsequential sound—but in the sudden stillness, it felt like the signal of a shift, a tipping point. "So... they can reopen cases?"

"In some situations," Ethan said, setting the paper down, though the gesture felt heavier than it should have. "If one party claims the process was unfair or incomplete."

Her heart began to beat in uneven pulses, and the edges of the room seemed to sharpen, as if the light and the space itself were suddenly too bright, too defined. Ethan was still speaking—something about the scope, the committees, the expected public hearings—but his voice had already faded into the background of her own spiraling thoughts.

August's name rose unbidden, like smoke curling from an ember she'd thought long extinguished. She hadn't spoken it in weeks—not since she'd begun to believe that their story had finally run its course—but now it came back like a chill in the bloodstream.

He could file something. He could claim he hadn't fully consented. He could use the Act to unearth what had already been buried, to drag her—and by extension Ethan—back into the machinery of things that should have stayed ended.

Her throat went dry, the kind of dryness that makes swallowing feel like a labor. Miles's quiet humming filled the space—a soft, distracted melody that children make when the world feels safe enough to ignore. And yet, it pierced her, both gentle and cruel, a reminder of the fragile new peace they had carved out. His peace was new. The last few months had been the first stretch of time where he hadn't woken in the night, asking where everyone had gone, eyes wide and searching.

Vanessa blinked, trying to anchor herself in the warm morning, the scent of cinnamon lingering in the air, the faint creak of Ethan's chair. But the feeling persisted, a knot in her chest that no sunlight, no coffee, no playful noise could entirely untangle.

"What happens," she said, her voice barely above a whisper, "if someone uses this Act to challenge an annulment that's already final?"

Ethan's head lifted, his expression tightening. "Vanessa."

"I'm serious," she said, her fingers tightening on the edge of the counter, the smooth surface pressing into her palms.

He met her eyes, steady, careful. "We don't know yet. And you don't even know if it applies to—"

"It does," she cut in quickly, the words spilling out before she could stop them. "Ours was under emotional grounds. 'Irreconcilable differences.' That's exactly what this means."

Miles rolled a toy car across the floor, the soft *vroom* sound punctuating the tense silence between them like a small, accidental alarm.

Ethan rose from the table, his chair creaking beneath him, the newspaper still spread out behind him like a battlefield of bureaucracy. "Vanessa."

But she had already turned away, leaning both hands on the counter, staring out the window at the yard beyond—the one Ethan had promised to plant herbs in when spring comes. Now, the trees stood bare, thin branches etched starkly against the pale morning sky. The wind rattled them faintly, a reminder of the world outside their fragile bubble.

"It's barely been a month," she whispered, more to herself than to him. "We just got here."

He came to stand behind her, the warmth of his body a quiet anchor. "You're not going back there," he said, his voice low, firm.

"You don't know that," she murmured, the words tasting bitter, brittle.

He hesitated, then reached for her hand, brushing her fingers gently with his own. "Hey," he said softly, waiting until she turned her gaze back to him. "I'm not letting this touch what we've built."

For a moment, the kitchen felt suspended in a delicate balance—the quiet hum of the morning, Miles' soft play, the lingering scent of cinnamon and coffee—but the shadow of the Act lingered like an uninvited guest, whispering that nothing in the past was ever truly buried.

Her lips parted, but no words came.

Ethan's thumb brushed the back of her hand in a quiet, steadying rhythm. "Whatever this is—whatever noise it stirs up—we'll handle it. Together."

Miles made a triumphant squeal from the floor. "He won!"

Vanessa blinked, briefly pulled from the fog. "Who did?"

"The hero," Miles said, looking up at her with a wide grin. "He saved everyone."

She smiled faintly, the gesture small and fragile, though her eyes didn't quite catch the light.

Ethan watched her, his presence grounding her like a subtle anchor. "You hear that?" he said quietly. "Already a good ending."

She nodded, trying to let that innocent, simple declaration settle in her chest. But the tightness remained, clinging stubbornly. Outside, the wind had picked up, scattering the last of the leaves across the lawn. The day no longer felt settled, as if the world itself were whispering that calm was temporary.

By the afternoon, Vanessa found herself alone in

the living room. The television was still on—the muted broadcast looping footage of talking heads and courthouse steps—but she didn't watch. She sat curled at the edge of the couch, elbows on her knees, the faint hum of the refrigerator the only sound anchoring her to the present.

Ethan had taken Miles out for a short walk, muttering something about "getting fresh air before the rain." She knew he'd done it to give her space, but space hadn't helped. If anything, it had made the echoes louder, letting her thoughts stretch unchecked.

She reached for her phone and scrolled through the headlines again. Every article used the same phrase: *restorative justice for broken unions.* Some quoted leaders calling it an act of mercy, a second chance for reconciliation. Others framed it as a bureaucratic intrusion into private life, a violation of boundaries that should never be reopened.

She read until the words blurred together, the letters spinning and colliding in a way that made her stomach churn. Finally, she set the phone down and rubbed her forehead, the pressure of worry pulsing through her temples. The room felt smaller now, the quiet deeper, as though the air itself held its breath, waiting for what would come next.

It was not just the idea of August filing a petition, though that thought alone made her stomach twist. It was the implication beneath it, the quiet weight pressing on her chest. Healing could be questioned. Someone else, a stranger in a robe or a clerk behind a desk, could decide whether she had been allowed to move on. The thought made the room feel smaller, the walls inching closer, the light from the window failing to reach the corners of her unease.

She closed her eyes. For a moment she was back in that small tribunal office years ago. The scent of old paper and polished wood, the faint hum of a heater struggling against winter's chill, it all returned with uncanny clarity. The clerk's tired voice asked if she was sure, each word measured and deliberate. The pen had trembled slightly in her hand as she signed. The relief that came afterward had been like the first breath after surfacing from deep water, a rush of air and freedom she had almost taken for granted. Now someone was trying to rewrite that air, to question the validity of the life she had fought to reclaim.

The click of the door opening drew her out of the memory. She straightened instinctively, her muscles tense until recognition softened her posture. Ethan stepped inside, carrying Miles on his hip. Both were damp from the drizzle outside, the smell of wet coats and rain clinging to them. Miles's cheeks were flushed, and his small hands clutched a leaf nearly the size of his head.

"Look what we found," Ethan said, his voice warm, carrying the casual pride of a father who had helped his son discover a tiny treasure. "A maple that refused to quit."

Miles giggled, his laughter bright and free. "It's red like fire!"

Vanessa smiled faintly, reaching out for the leaf. "That's beautiful, sweetheart."

He handed it to her with a small flourish, a ceremony that seemed entirely natural to him, then wriggled down to return to his toys, the sound of his tiny feet tapping on the floor soft and rhythmic.

Ethan set the umbrella aside and hung his coat, the faint scent of rain lingering around him. "He wanted to show you before it got dark," he said.

Vanessa nodded, tracing the veins of the leaf with her thumb. Its color was almost impossibly vivid, a reminder that life persisted even in the smallest corners. Ethan watched her for a long moment, as though weighing whether to disturb the fragile calm. Finally, he spoke. "You have been sitting here since we left," he said quietly, his tone gentle but insistent.

She met his eyes, feeling the weight of their shared understanding, the unspoken acknowledgment that the outside world had intruded and that she needed to breathe through it, one moment at a time.

She did not look up. "I've been reading."

"I can tell." He moved closer, lowering himself into the armchair opposite her, the familiar creak of the cushions under his weight grounding the moment. "You're trying to find something that will make it less terrifying."

"That's not—" She stopped, her words caught in the brittle edge of someone who had spent the day pretending to be calm. "It's not about fear. It's about what happens next."

"Nothing happens next," Ethan said evenly, his voice steady, deliberate. "Not unless someone makes it happen."

She finally met his gaze. "You mean if August makes it happen."

He hesitated, then nodded slowly. "Yeah."

She laughed softly, the sound almost disbelieving. "He would. You know he would."

"Maybe," Ethan said, a trace of caution in his tone. "But maybe not. People change."

Her eyes locked onto his, the conviction in her expression startling even her. "He doesn't."

The weight of her words carried the memory of years that had left marks even after time had softened them. Ethan leaned forward, elbows resting on his knees, the quiet hum of the house wrapping around them.

"Okay," he said softly. "Say he does. Say he files something. Then what?"

She opened her mouth, then closed it again, unsure

of what to say.

"Then we show up," Ethan continued, calm and patient. "Together. You tell your story. I tell mine. We let the truth stand on its own legs."

She shook her head, the motion slow, deliberate. "It's not that simple. Once the process starts, it's all out of our hands, in the hands of lawyers, boards, the press. Everyone has a say except the people it actually happened to."

He did not interrupt. He let the silence stretch, the only sounds the faint hum of the refrigerator and the occasional distant call of a bird outside the window. She drew in a slow breath, and finally, her gaze returned to him.

"You built this," she said softly, voice trembling with a mixture of gratitude and fear. "This peace. I don't want to drag you through that."

Ethan reached across the space between them and brushed her hand with his, steady and unshakable. "You will not," he said quietly, the certainty in his tone as solid as the walls around them. "We face it together. Always together."

For a moment, the world outside their living room faded, leaving only the hum of the house, the vivid color of the maple leaf in her hand from earlier, and the quiet certainty of shared strength.

"You're not dragging anything," he said, his voice calm, steady, the kind of calm she had always envied in him. "And I knew, from the moment I asked you to marry me, that your past wasn't a door that would stay sealed forever. But we are not the same people anymore. That is the difference."

Vanessa leaned back, letting her shoulders sink into the couch, the fabric soft beneath her. "I don't want Miles to see it. Any of it. He is just learning what normal feels like."

Ethan's expression softened, the faint curve of a smile touching his lips. "Then we keep showing him normal, as best we can."

Her gaze fell to the floor, where Miles was arranging his toys in a perfect line, his tiny hands moving with deliberate care. The sight hit her with a tenderness so fierce it almost hurt, a quiet ache she could barely name. He was humming again, lost in his own small world, blissfully unaware of the tremors beneath the surface, the invisible weight pressing against her chest.

"How do you explain something like this to a child?" she murmured, her voice barely carrying above the soft rhythm of the rain against the window.

"You don't," Ethan said gently, the tone even, patient. "You just live the truth loud enough that he can feel it."

Her throat tightened, a small, stubborn lump that made swallowing difficult. "And if the world doesn't let us?"

"Then we make our own world," he said simply. There was a quiet confidence in the way he spoke, a certainty that felt like a shield around her heart.

The room filled again with the small, domestic sounds that had become the markers of their new normal. Miles's toys clattered softly as he rearranged them once more, the ticking of the clock punctuated the quiet, and the faint patter of rain outside tapped gently against the window. The muted voice of the news anchor murmured from the television, reporting tribunals and hearings, but it was a distant, impersonal noise that belonged to someone else's world.

Ethan stood and reached for the remote, turning the television off.

"Enough noise," he said, his tone soft but firm, filling the room with a sense of order and calm.

Vanessa let out a slow breath, the tension in her chest loosening just slightly, though she knew the worry would not vanish entirely. For a moment, she allowed herself to simply watch Miles at play, to feel the pulse of ordinary life steady beneath the shadows that lingered at the edges.

The sudden silence was almost startling. Vanessa let out a long breath she hadn't realized she was holding, the sound dissolving quietly into the calm of the room. Ethan came to sit beside her, the soft scrape of the couch cushion against the floor a gentle reminder that he was there. He reached for her hand, and she didn't resist, allowing the warmth and steadiness of his presence to anchor her.

"You're safe," he said quietly, his voice low and sure, as though the words themselves could push the shadows back.

She closed her eyes. "Say it again."

"You're safe," he repeated, slower this time, each word deliberate, wrapping around her like a blanket.

It did not erase the fear, but it gave it boundaries, turned it into something she could hold rather than drown in, a shape she could name and place.

Miles climbed onto the couch between them, a toy in each hand, cheeks flushed from the last traces of the evening chill. "Can he stay here?" he asked, holding up a little figure with triumphant pride.

Ethan smiled, the corners of his eyes crinkling. "Sure. Plenty of room."

Vanessa pulled Miles closer, resting her chin against his soft hair, inhaling the faint scent of shampoo and the lingering warmth of his body. She glanced at Ethan, who met her gaze without words, a quiet understanding passing between them. For now, it was enough.

Night came softly, as if it did not want to intrude, tucking the world in with shadows that felt protective rather than ominous. Miles had fallen asleep between them after dinner, one hand curled around the stuffed dinosaur Ethan had rescued from the laundry earlier, the small rise and fall of his chest a gentle rhythm in the room. Vanessa carried him to bed, careful not to disturb the peaceful curve of his body, and tucked the blanket around his shoulders. She lingered there longer than usual, brushing a stray strand of hair from his head, memorizing the quiet perfection of this moment.

Downstairs, she could hear Ethan clearing the last of the dishes, the clink of ceramic and soft hum of running water blending into the ambient hush of the house. When she joined him, he was standing by the sink, drying his hands on a towel. The kitchen light was dim, casting a soft amber glow that pooled over the counters, warming the room and making it feel smaller, intimate, and contained. She leaned against the counter, letting the warmth and quiet settle around her like a gentle shield, listening to the last rhythms of the day before darkness fully claimed the house.

"Is he out?" Ethan asked, his voice low, careful.

"Completely," she replied, a small sigh escaping her lips.

He smiled faintly, the kind of quiet, private smile that carried reassurance without needing words. "That's something."

She nodded, leaning against the doorway, her body relaxing just a little. "You were right about the leaf. He loved it."

Ethan turned slightly, resting his back against the counter, the dim kitchen light casting warm shadows across his features. "You okay?"

She hesitated. It was a simple question, yet it carried a weight far too large to fit inside simple answers.

"I keep thinking about the wording," she said finally, her voice low, almost fragile. "How they call it the Restore Building Bridges Act, like it's something beautiful."

"Politicians love names that sound like healing," Ethan said dryly, but there was no bite in his tone, just observation.

She crossed her arms, a small motion of frustration and disbelief. "It's the opposite. It's not restoring anything. It's reopening."

He nodded slowly, his gaze steady. "Yeah."

She looked up at him, her expression open, searching. "Do you ever feel like every time I take a step forward, something comes back to test it?"

Ethan didn't answer right away. He walked over, his steps quiet on the floor, and brushed a thumb along her jaw, soft and deliberate. "Maybe," he said quietly. "Or maybe it's the same storm showing up in new clothes."

The line might have sounded poetic coming from anyone else, but from him, it felt grounding, as if he had named the chaos and made it manageable. She leaned into his touch for a moment, eyes half-closed, letting herself exist in the small certainty of him.

They stayed like that for a while, the silence around them filled with subtle, domestic sounds—the faint hum of the refrigerator, the muted tick of the clock, the soft padding of rain against the windows. Later, they moved to sit together at the table, just the two of them, letting the world wait outside. Words were not needed. The simple act of being present, of sharing the quiet, was enough.

"When I signed the annulment," she said, her voice low, almost a murmur, "I thought it was the last time I would have to explain myself to anyone. I didn't think there could ever be a reason to justify that kind of ending again."

"You don't have to justify it," Ethan said, his voice quiet but firm, a gentle insistence that it was true even when the world might not agree.

"I might." Her eyes flicked toward the folded newspaper on the counter, its stark letters an uninvited reminder of the threat lingering in the background. "If this becomes real, I might have to explain every decision I made—why I left, how I healed, why I believed it was done."

Ethan reached across the table, his hand warm over hers, grounding her in the present. "Then you will tell the truth. That's all you owe anyone."

She exhaled slowly, letting the tension seep from her shoulders in a tiny, deliberate release. "You make it sound simple."

"It isn't," he said, his gaze steady, unwavering. "But it's enough."

Outside, rain began to fall, soft and steady, tapping against the window in a quiet rhythm. Vanessa stood and walked to the glass, pressing her fingers to the cold pane. Streetlights glowed through the drizzle, their reflections running down the glass like fragile threads of light. Somewhere beyond that glass, the rest of the world continued, talking, arguing about laws, broadcasting opinions, dissecting lives that were not theirs to dissect.

She turned slightly, her voice low and uncertain. "You think he's seen the news?"

"Probably," Ethan said, his tone measured, acknowledging the truth without adding weight to it.

She nodded once, the gesture small but determined. "He'll take it as a sign."

Ethan joined her at the window, moving close enough that she could feel the warmth from his arm against hers. "Then let him. It doesn't change who you are," he said softly, a quiet anchor in the storm of her thoughts.

Vanessa wanted to believe him. She leaned against the window, letting the rain wash over the world outside while she tried to let it touch her inside. But beneath the calm, something old and familiar stirred— the part of her that remembered how quickly peace could unravel when someone else decided they wanted a say. The thought brushed against her like a cold wind, and she closed her eyes for a moment, clutching the warmth of Ethan's presence like a shield.

She turned to him, her voice quiet but firm. "If he does something, if he files a claim or contacts anyone, I want to be the one who tells Miles. On my terms."

Ethan nodded. "Of course."

She looked back out at the rain sliding down the window, the streetlights casting pale, trembling reflections across the wet pavement. "I don't want him growing up thinking the past can just reach out and rewrite itself."

Ethan was quiet for a long moment, letting her words hang in the air. Then he said, softly, almost as if speaking to the rhythm of the falling rain, "He won't. Because he's watching you."

Vanessa met his eyes. The weight in them, the quiet certainty, steadied something inside her. He wrapped an arm around her waist, and she let herself lean into him, pressing her forehead against his shoulder. For a while, neither spoke. The rain outside softened to a gentle whisper, threading through the quiet of the house.

The newspaper still lay open on the table. Its bold headline caught the faint light spilling from the hallway:

"Restore Building Bridges Act Passes — Tribunals Begin Monday."

A drop of water from the damp air had smudged the ink slightly, blurring the word *restore* so that only *building bridges* remained clear. By morning, that phrase would be everywhere—on television panels, in sermons, in the conversations of neighbors who meant well but did not understand. Tonight, though, it was only paper and silence, a small, fragile moment before the world intruded.

Vanessa paused in the doorway, her fingers brushing the edge of the table, lingering over the shadow of the words. She let the light fade and the silence settle around her like a cloak. Then she turned off the kitchen light. The darkness seemed to absorb the headline, erasing it from the room while leaving its weight behind in her chest. She climbed the stairs slowly, each step measured, carrying the quiet tension with her, the knowledge of what was coming beginning to take shape like a stone settling in the hollow of her ribs.

CHAPTER 15

The RRB Act

The letter arrived on a Wednesday. At first glance, it seemed ordinary—a plain off-white envelope with a faint embossed seal of the Ecclesiastical and Civil Restorative Review Board in the corner. The kind of envelope that might carry a donation receipt or a notice about taxes. But the return address made her hand freeze: Office of Marital Review, Department of Faith and Civil Affairs—Washington, D.C.

Vanessa lingered in the entryway, one hand still gripping the door that had clicked shut behind the postman. Her chest tightened. Her heart had already begun its uneven climb toward panic. She set the rest of the mail on the console—a utility bill, a coupon flyer, a letter from her mother adorned with a cheerful stamp—but couldn't bring herself to set down the envelope. It felt heavier than paper should, a tangible weight of consequence.

Her thumb traced the embossed seal, rough and slightly raised against her skin. She could almost hear her pulse in the quiet hallway, the faint ticking of the wall clock marking time she didn't want to measure. This was real. This was happening.

Ethan's voice floated from the kitchen, casual, unaware. "You want another coffee?"

She didn't answer. The words lodged somewhere between her throat and her chest.

A moment later, he stepped into the entryway, sleeves rolled to his forearms, droplets of water still clinging to the ends of his damp hair. "Vanessa?"

Her eyes didn't leave the envelope. His frown deepened. "What's that?"

She hesitated, a flicker of fear mingling with disbelief. How could a single piece of paper—just paper—carry enough power to change everything? Her fingers tightened around it, crumpling the edges slightly, and she felt the surge of a thousand possibilities, none of them certain, most of them terrifying.

Ethan stepped closer, his shadow stretching across the polished wood floor. "Vanessa, talk to me."

Finally, her voice emerged, low and uneven. "It's... from the Office of Marital Review."

The words seemed to hang in the air between them, heavier than the envelope itself. Ethan's brow furrowed further. "The...?"

She swallowed hard, as if the next sentence might break the fragile calm of the house. "They're reviewing... everything."

She didn't speak. Her fingers lingered on the envelope as if touching it might delay the inevitable. Slowly, almost without conscious thought, she turned it over, staring at her own name printed in that stark, bureaucratic block font. The letters looked foreign, somehow claiming a piece of her she didn't want to surrender.

Then, almost instinctively, she slid her finger under

the flap. The paper tore softly, a sound too gentle for the weight of what it carried. She unfolded the letter, holding it with both hands as if it might shatter if released.

At first, the words swam before her eyes: notification of review… annulment dated… pursuant to Section 4B of the Restore Building Bridges Act…

Her vision sharpened on a single, piercing line:

"Your prior annulment has been selected for review pending verification of mutual consent."

Her breath caught. She read it again. The words didn't change.

"Vanessa?" Ethan's voice came closer, tentative, cautious.

She handed him the page, unable to summon sound from her throat. His eyes scanned the letter quickly, the crease in his forehead deepening with each line.

"This is—" He stopped, swallowing. "They're actually doing it."

Her hands trembled, the paper quivering between them. "It says selected for review… What does that even mean?"

Ethan chose his words carefully, as if measuring them against the tension in the room. "It means... someone—probably August—filed an appeal."

The name struck her like a blow she hadn't felt coming, reverberating through the fragile stillness she'd tried to cling to. Her chest tightened. "No," she whispered. "He wouldn't—"

But even as the words left her mouth, they felt hollow, a fragile denial against the reality that had already crept through the walls of her life. Of course he would find a way to stretch his shadow across the years, reaching into corners she had thought were safe.

Ethan looked up from the letter. "You don't know it's him."

"Who else would it be?" she said quietly. "It's not like they pick random people out of kindness."

He folded the paper once, too neatly. "We'll talk to someone. Find out what this actually means before we panic."

Before we panic. The words should have been comforting. But something in his tone made her feel suddenly alone.

She turned away, walking toward the kitchen without answering. The kettle still sat on the counter from breakfast. She reached for it, needing to do something. Her hands moved automatically, filling, pouring, switching on—the same motions she had done a thousand times before.

Behind her, Ethan said quietly, "You don't have to read into it. We'll get clarity."

Her laugh came out sharp. "Clarity? Ethan, it says they're reviewing my annulment. That is not unclear. That is my past, rewritten in the mail."

He was silent for a moment. "I'm just saying, don't let fear decide what it means yet."

She turned to face him. "You're already talking like it's not happening."

"I'm talking like we should breathe before we drown," he said.

The kettle began to hum. She stared at him, searching for something—anger, fear, anything that matched what was spiraling inside her. But his face remained calm, steady, almost impossibly so.

"It's not about panic," she said finally, her voice tight. "It's about reality. Someone out there is deciding whether our marriage even counts."

Ethan opened his mouth, then closed it again. His silence landed heavier than any argument, filling the space between them with something unspoken, a weight she could feel pressing against her chest.

The sharp thud of Miles's footsteps came down the stairs, breaking the moment. "Mama! The pirate fell into the volcano!"

Vanessa forced her voice to remain steady. "Oh no, poor pirate."

He grinned, waving the small action figure triumphantly. "He'll climb out!"

Ethan managed a small smile for him, the effort faint but real. "You've got a brave pirate there, buddy."

Miles raced past them into the living room, humming a tune he had made up, completely oblivious to the tension he left behind. Vanessa poured the hot water over the tea bag, the steam curling upward in delicate ribbons. She watched the mist blur the reflection in the kettle's curved metal and realized the person staring back at her seemed unfamiliar—tight-lipped, wide-eyed, someone holding her own panic behind a mask of composure.

Ethan set the letter down on the counter, his hands lingering near it as if to anchor them both. "We'll handle this," he said quietly.

She didn't look at him. "You keep saying we, like it's not my name on that letter."

He flinched, the brief flicker of hurt crossing his face. "That's not fair," he said softly.

"Neither is this," she said, her voice trembling despite her efforts to steady it. "But it's happening anyway."

The kettle began to hum more insistently, filling the kitchen with a mundane, domestic sound that contrasted sharply with the storm raging inside her. She poured the tea into her cup, feeling the warmth through the porcelain, but it did little to settle the cold knot in her stomach. Her hands shook slightly as she carried the cup to the counter, setting it down beside the letter. The ordinary world of morning routines, of steaming tea and a laughing child, felt impossibly fragile, hanging by a thread over the decisions of people she would never meet.

Ethan watched her, his jaw tight, his expression unreadable for a long moment. Then he reached out, brushing a loose strand of hair from her face. "We'll figure this out. Together," he said, and though his words were calm, Vanessa could hear the unspoken acknowledgment that the path ahead would not be easy.

She nodded, not trusting herself to speak. The letter sat between them, a cold, flat reminder that the past had never truly let her go, and the future was suddenly uncertain. Miles's laughter floated up from the living room, a fragile thread of normalcy that neither of them could ignore.

The kettle clicked off. The sound was final, like a door closing. The letter stayed on the counter all morning, lying between the fruit bowl and the folded newspaper, as if it were radioactive. The postmark read Tuesday, 2:08 p.m. Yesterday afternoon. That meant by the time she and Ethan had been watching the rain together, talking softly in the kitchen, this letter was already on its way. Her old life traveling through the postal system while she had been saying things like *you're safe.*

The next day, after breakfast, she sat at the kitchen counter, staring at the envelope as if its presence could somehow alter what it contained. The worst hadn't even begun, and yet her reality was already cracking. She wished the past would stay in the past. She wished August would finally allow her to breathe without the constant fear of losing everything she had built.

Ethan appeared in the doorway a moment later, phone in hand. "Everything okay?"

"Fine," she said, not meeting his eyes.

He hesitated, studying her. "You sure?"

She nodded once, too quickly. "Your meeting done?"

"Just finished. They're restructuring the committee again."

She gave a thin smile, one that didn't reach her eyes. "Seems to be a theme lately."

He frowned slightly, not catching the edge in her tone. "You should eat something."

"I'm not hungry," she replied, her voice quieter than she intended. She traced a finger along the edge of the envelope, the paper still stiff from being unfolded, a fragile tether to a past she thought she had left behind.

He leaned against the doorway frame, studying her. "You've been standing there for an hour."

"So?"

"So... maybe sit. Take a walk. Do something that isn't staring at that letter."

Her head snapped up. "You think I want to be staring at it?"

"That's not what I meant."

"But it's what you said."

Ethan ran a hand through his hair, exhaling slowly. "Vanessa—"

She turned away, rinsing the cloth in the sink, the sound of water hitting porcelain sharp in the quiet kitchen. "You act like it's just another problem to solve. Like if we schedule it right, it won't hurt as much."

His jaw tightened. "I'm trying to keep us grounded."

"By pretending it's fine?"

"By not letting it eat us alive before we even know what it is," he said, his voice steady but tinged with worry.

She laughed, bitterly. "You're already calling it it, not this. Like it's happening to someone else."

Miles came into the kitchen, clutching a picture he had drawn, bright streaks of blue and orange leaping across the paper. "Mama, look! It's us!"

She knelt automatically, forcing herself to shift focus. "That's beautiful, sweetheart."

He pointed to the tallest figure on the page. "That's Daddy. He's building the bridge so we can cross."

Ethan smiled faintly, the first trace of warmth since the letter arrived. "That's a pretty strong bridge."

Miles nodded with solemn pride. "It doesn't fall, even if the wind comes."

Vanessa swallowed hard. The coincidence made her throat ache, the metaphor cutting sharper than she expected. She looked down at Miles, his little hands gripping the paper, eyes bright with trust and faith she wasn't sure she could fully match. "That's good," she managed. "That's very good."

Her gaze flicked to Ethan, who was watching her with careful attention, silently reminding her that even as her past threatened to intrude, this moment—this family—still mattered. The letter lay on the counter, heavy and unyielding, but for the first time that morning, the weight in her chest felt slightly shared, not entirely hers to carry.

When Miles ran off again, the quiet returned. It felt heavier now, charged with the echo of the word *bridge*, lingering in the kitchen like smoke.

Ethan glanced toward the drawing. "He hears more than we think."

Vanessa crossed her arms, pressing herself into the moment. "Then maybe we should start saying things that actually make sense."

"Vanessa…"

She shook her head, frustration threading her voice. "You keep saying we'll handle it. But do you even believe that? Or are you just hoping that if you sound calm enough, I'll stop being scared?"

His mouth opened, then closed again. The truth

was he didn't know how to answer without making it worse.

She turned back to the counter, tracing the edge of the letter absentmindedly. "I can't do silence again, Ethan. Not like before."

"I'm not being silent," he said quietly, voice low but steady.

"You are," she said, turning to face him. "You're just filling the space with calm words. That's still silence."

He stepped closer, the tension in his shoulders easing only slightly. "What do you want me to say?"

"I want you to feel it," she said, the words trembling. "To let it hit you. Because it hit me the second I saw my name on that page."

He stared at her, the struggle visible in the line of his jaw, in the way his eyes darkened for just a moment. "If I let it hit me, one of us has to stay standing."

Her eyes stung, but she met his gaze. "Then maybe I don't want to be the one who falls."

They stood like that for a long moment, the soft hum of Miles's voice drifting from the other room, the ordinary rhythm of childhood pressing against the ache of adult fear.

Finally, Ethan exhaled, a long, measured breath. "You're right. I don't know what to say that doesn't make it worse. But I'm still here."

Vanessa let the words settle around them. He didn't have all the answers. He didn't have to. Being here, standing together, made the weight of the letter just slightly more bearable.

She nodded, but it was not agreement. "Being here isn't the same as standing with me."

He looked down, then back at her. "I know."

A moment later, he left the room. The quiet that followed was heavier than shouting would have been. Vanessa sank into a chair, her eyes fixed on the letter once again. The paper seemed to breathe in the morning light, edges softening and sharpening all at once. She reached out, tracing the embossed seal with her fingertip until the lines blurred beneath her touch.

Selected for review. The phrase echoed in her mind.

Selected, as if she were part of a lottery she had never entered.

Review, as if her life were an essay being graded by some unseen authority.

In the reflection of the kitchen window, she saw her own pale face staring back at her, hollowed with worry. Behind her, the dining table was still cluttered with proof of ordinary life: crayons, coffee rings, a half-eaten slice of toast. Proof that this home had existed before the letter arrived. And yet, everything looked different now, as if the envelope had changed the color of the air itself.

Her thoughts drifted to August. She imagined his hands holding the same kind of envelope, his quiet, controlled smile curling into satisfaction. He had always said endings were illusions. That people only pretended to move on. Her stomach tightened, a cold, twisting knot. She could almost hear his voice whispering in her mind, taunting, calculating.

Vanessa pressed her palms flat against the table until her knuckles ached, as if grounding herself in the solid surface could anchor her against the rising panic. "Not this time," she whispered, her voice low but fierce. She would not let him touch her life again, not through fear, not through bureaucracy, not through memories she had tried to bury.

The next morning, she woke before dawn. Ethan was asleep beside her, one arm draped over the edge of the bed. She lay there for a long moment, watching the slow rhythm of his breathing. It used to calm her, but now it stirred a faint panic she couldn't name. Perhaps calm had become a mask for denial. Perhaps she no longer trusted silence.

When the first thin line of light appeared at the window, she slipped out of bed, careful not to wake him.

Downstairs, the letter still sat on the counter where she had left it, the official seal broken, its contents folded neatly inside. She had not read it again since yesterday. She did not need to. Every word was already memorized:

This correspondence is to inform you that the annulment of your previous marriage, filed under grounds of emotional incompatibility, has been selected for review under the Restore Building Bridges Act (RBB Act §12.4b). The review process may involve testimonial reassessment and witness verification to ensure due consent and the legitimacy of the dissolution. Parties involved: Vanessa Claire Pepper (now Sinclair) and August Nathaniel Pepper.

The way the names sat together—one old, one current—made her skin crawl. It was like reading her own obituary, written by someone who believed they knew her better than she knew herself.

She ran her thumb over the word *review*. On paper, it looked harmless, innocuous even. But she knew what it meant in practice: exposure. She would be forced to revisit every fracture in her past, to prove again that what had broken was truly broken. To show that the loneliness, the control, and the emotional suffocation she had endured were not imagined. And worse, that she had not sinned by trying to heal.

Her stomach knotted, a low, insistent tension that spread through her chest. The morning light fell across the countertop, illuminating the paper as if daring her to face it again. She wanted to turn away, to ignore it, to leave the letter untouched, but she could not. It was a summons, a summons that demanded recognition.

When Ethan came downstairs an hour later, she was sitting at the table, hands wrapped around an untouched cup of coffee. The rich aroma filled the kitchen, but she had not taken a sip.

He hesitated in the doorway. "Did you sleep?"

"Some," she said quietly, eyes still on the dark liquid in front of her.

He nodded. "Any updates from the office?"

"No."

Silence stretched between them, thick and uncomfortable. Then he said, "I've been saying for the past few days that we should talk to someone. It will help."

She looked up sharply. "Someone?"

"Legal counsel, maybe. Or our pastor—"

"No," she interrupted, her voice firm.

He blinked. "Why not?"

"Because it's exactly what they want. For us to turn it into a process, not a wound."

Ethan exhaled slowly, running a hand over his face. "Ness, it is a process. And if we don't handle it right, they'll just—"

"They'll what?" she cut in. "Reinstate a marriage that doesn't exist?"

His voice softened, steady but weighed with worry. "That's what we have to prevent."

She stared at him for a long moment, disbelief and frustration warring in her chest. "Do you even hear how absurd that sounds? Preventing my past from happening again?"

The words hung in the kitchen, fragile and sharp, a reminder of how completely her life had been upended by a single piece of paper. Ethan's gaze did not waver, but she could see the tension coiled in his shoulders, the quiet acknowledgment that this was no ordinary problem they could schedule and solve.

Ethan rubbed his temple, his fingers pressing into the tension there. "I'm trying to protect us."

"By treating me like a case file?"

"By making sure this doesn't destroy everything we've built."

She laughed once, a short, sharp sound. "You mean the part of our life that looks calm from the outside."

He looked wounded but said nothing.

Vanessa leaned back in her chair. "You know what this is really about?" she asked quietly. "It's about the system asking if I'm sure. If I were really certain when I walked away. As if trauma needs to fill out a form."

Ethan stayed silent.

"They think forgiveness means returning," she went on, her voice steady but tight. "That healing looks like restoration. But what if healing is staying gone?"

He opened his mouth, but she continued. "When August and I ended things, the court said we were incompatible. But that word—" She shook her head. "It doesn't capture every decision, every emotion, filtered through his control until I couldn't hear myself anymore."

Her hands trembled slightly as she gripped the edge of the table. "And now they're asking me to revisit that? To sit in front of some tribunal and explain why it wasn't love? As if I didn't already bleed that answer once?"

Ethan came closer, crouching beside her chair, his hand brushing the back of hers. "You don't have to go through it alone."

She stared at him, searching his eyes for conviction. "Then say it, Ethan. Say you believe this is wrong."

He hesitated, a fraction too long, and the pause said everything she needed to know. Vanessa looked away, the weight of his silence pressing down. "You're scared of choosing sides," she said quietly, her voice laced with hurt.

"I'm scared of losing you to this," he said quietly.

"You don't lose someone by standing beside them," she replied, her voice firm but measured.

He rested a hand lightly on her arm. "I'm here."

She didn't pull away, but she didn't reach back either. "Being here isn't enough if you're standing behind me."

For a long time, neither of them moved. The house creaked as it warmed, the soft noises of morning filling the silence between them. A bird struck the window lightly and flew off again. Somewhere upstairs, Miles laughed in his sleep, a tiny bubble of normalcy in a world that already felt off-kilter.

Vanessa finally stood, leaving her coffee untouched. "I need air."

Ethan rose as well. "Want me to come?"

She shook her head. "Not yet."

Outside, the sky was pale and thin, almost washed-out in the early light. The neighborhood looked unchanged. Lawns glistened with early dew, mailboxes stood upright, and dogs barked faintly in the distance.

She walked down the street barefoot, the pavement cool and firm against her skin, a grounding sensation that contrasted sharply with the turmoil in her chest. Each step reminded her that the world was moving forward, indifferent to the upheaval she carried inside. She imagined men in suits, sitting around polished tables, discussing her emotions as if they were exhibits in a case file. The thought made her stomach twist, the absurdity and intrusion of it fueling a quiet, simmering anger.

The morning air smelled of wet grass and possibility, but even that felt tainted, filtered through the lens of what the letter demanded of her. She clenched her fists briefly, testing the strength she would need to meet it head-on.

"Did she consent to the annulment?"

"Was she of sound judgment?"

"Was her desire to remarry influenced by emotional instability?"

By the time she reached the edge of the block, her hands were shaking. She pressed them to her chest, trying to slow her racing heartbeat, trying to pull her scattered thoughts back into something manageable.

For a moment, she pictured August seated calmly at some hearing table. He would smile that half-sympathetic smile, the one that always made people think he was the wronged one. *I only wanted what was best for her,* she could hear him saying. *She was never herself after everything that happened in Antigua. I tried to help her heal, but she was emotionally gone.*

She clenched her fists and took a slow, measured breath, shutting her eyes. She could not allow August to touch her peace again. She could not let him rewrite her life through the judgments of strangers.

Her chest rose and fell with deliberate rhythm, a tether to the present. She would not let fear decide this moment. She had to fight. She was determined to fight.

The morning air, cool against her bare feet, no

longer felt indifferent. It felt like something she could lean into, a quiet ally against the chaos waiting in that letter.

CHAPTER 16

Forgiveness Is Not a Return

The letter sat crumpled in her hand, its edges damp from the sweat she hadn't realized she was producing. Vanessa only noticed how tightly she'd gripped it when Ethan reached across the gearshift and covered her hand with his own.

"We don't have to talk," he said softly.

She nodded once, her gaze fixed on the building ahead. It wasn't exactly a courthouse—not like the ones she remembered from civics class—but a hybrid tribunal. Its limestone facade carried both the seal of the state and the crest of the Church Council of Restoration, their emblems carved side by side above the archway. The sight made her skin crawl.

This was the new face of law under the Restore Broken Bridges Act, where civil annulments and divorces could be re-examined if deemed "non-biblical" or "unsubstantiated." And, of course, hers had been singled out for review, deemed eligible for reconciliation.

Vanessa swallowed, feeling the weight of the letter like a stone in her chest. Every step she took toward that building felt like walking deeper into a world that no longer belonged to her. The air seemed heavier here, charged with authority and expectation, and she couldn't tell if it was the law, the Church, or her own memories that made her pulse race.

She let out a dry laugh. "Reconciliation potential," she murmured, as if tasting poison. Ethan squeezed her hand once more, but she didn't look at him. The last two weeks had stretched them thin, like a thread pulled to its last fiber. He had stood by her, calm and rational as always, while she paced their living room, running through every angle August could exploit, imagining every word and gesture.

"Are you ready?" he asked.

"No," she admitted honestly, pushing the car door open. "But I'm here."

Inside, the hallway smelled of old wood polish and faint incense. An usher in a navy blazer checked their names against a clipboard and handed Vanessa a beige badge stamped with a barcode and a number—Respondent #42. She slid it into her coat pocket. She had a name, and yet, here, she was just a number.

The tribunal chamber felt like a chapel married to a courtroom. Pews had been replaced with rigid chairs, but the stained-glass windows remained, casting fractured light across the room. A crucifix hung on the back wall above the judges' bench, the figure of Christ watching over them as if to remind all present that forgiveness was the priority.

Ethan guided her to the respondent's table. His hand was steady, a quiet anchor against her tremors. Across the aisle, August was already seated. He looked cleaner than ever during their marriage. His suit was perfectly pressed, hair immaculately combed, and a Bible lay open on the table in front of him. He wore the mask of humility well, but Vanessa could see the effort beneath it, the careful rehearsal of the image he wanted them to believe.

When their eyes met, he gave her that same calm, almost apologetic smile. She wanted to scream at him—if he truly felt sorry, they wouldn't be here. He wouldn't have barged back into her life unbidden.

The tribunal cleric announced that the session would begin shortly. Vanessa sank into her chair, her heart hammering against her ribs. The tribunal bell rang twice, sharp and echoing, and three members of the Review Board filed in through the side door, each dressed in cream-colored robes trimmed with deep green bands.

The lead member, a man in his sixties with silver hair combed meticulously back, carried a leather-bound Bible in one hand and a sheaf of documents in the other. Vanessa watched silently as they took their seats behind the long, raised desk.

"Session for Case #RBB–42 is now in order," the clerk announced. "Review of the annulment between August Nathaniel Pepper and Vanessa Claire Pepper—currently Sinclair. Grounds: emotional incompatibility and irreconcilable differences. Annulment approved under civil and church jurisdiction."

The lead reviewer adjusted his glasses. "The purpose of this hearing," he began, "is to determine whether the annulment in question was filed and approved under biblical grounds, and to assess, under the Restore Broken Bridges Act, whether reconciliation measures should be mandated."

Reconciliation measures. Vanessa's stomach clenched. It was a carefully sterile phrase that really meant: Can the state and the Church force you to face what you spent years escaping?

Another panel member, a woman with a soft face and sharp eyes, leaned toward the microphone. "Let the record show both parties are present. Counsel for the petitioner?"

A young man in a navy suit stood. He couldn't have been more than thirty-five. His voice was calm, measured, but Vanessa heard the practiced rhythm beneath the smooth delivery.

"Counselor Avery Grant, representing Mr. Pepper. My client has filed this petition in good faith, under the tenets of Matthew 5:23–24, which calls the faithful to reconcile with their estranged brother or sister before laying offerings at the altar. He seeks restoration, not retaliation."

"Counsel for the respondent?"

Vanessa's lawyer, Nadia Okafor, rose with effortless composure. She was one of the few people Vanessa trusted to speak in rooms like this. They hadn't been in touch for years, but their friendship from university had endured, and Nadia's professionalism radiated calm reassurance. Reuniting under these circumstances was awkward, but Vanessa had no one else she could rely on.

"Nadia Okafor, representing Mrs. Sinclair. My client is here under protest. She stands by the original grounds of the annulment, which were lawfully reviewed, verified, and finalized five years ago."

The lead reviewer nodded. "Acknowledged. We will begin with opening statements. Petitioner's side first."

Vanessa's chest tightened as August rose. He hadn't changed much in five years. If anything, he had perfected the image of gentle regret. He held the Bible lightly in one hand, like a man holding an heirloom, not a weapon, yet the weight of its presence in the room pressed on her anyway.

"Thank you, honorable members of the board," he began. His voice was steady, carrying just enough humility to sound holy. "I won't stand here and claim perfection. Our marriage… faltered. We both made mistakes. But it was never broken beyond repair. We loved each other once, and love—true love—isn't disposable. It doesn't vanish because it becomes inconvenient."

A few heads in the room nodded faintly. Vanessa clenched her jaw, resisting the familiar churn in her stomach.

"I believe," August continued, "that in our haste, in a moment of anger, decisions were made that did not honor God's design for marriage. I did not contest the annulment then because I believed time and prayer would bring clarity, and it has. I have spent these years rebuilding my faith, counseling with my church, and I now stand here with the conviction that what God joined together was not meant to be torn apart by the state."

Vanessa stared straight ahead. She didn't need to look at him to feel the familiar press of his words—the way they always sought to make her resistance seem like rebellion, her pain a misunderstanding.

"I do not stand here to control anyone," he said, the picture of sincerity. "I stand here to heal what was wounded. To offer forgiveness and restoration. I believe in Vanessa. I believe in us."

The board member with sharp eyes gave a small approving nod, as though she had heard something righteous.

"Respondent?" the lead reviewer prompted.

Nadia stood—Vanessa didn't, not yet.

"Mrs. Sinclair's position is simple. This matter was settled five years ago. The state and church both acknowledged that reconciliation was not possible. She has since rebuilt her life, remarried, and moved on. This retroactive review undermines not only her dignity, but also the finality of due legal process. We reject the idea that spiritual obligation should override individual safety and autonomy."

A soft murmur rippled through the room; some nodded in agreement, while others shifted in their seats, uneasy with the frankness.

The lead reviewer raised his hand. "This is not a political debate. We are here to assess biblical and legal grounds. Let us proceed."

As the tribunal moved into the formal testimonies, Vanessa felt her pulse thrum against her throat. This wasn't a courtroom. It was a confession booth disguised as one. Today, they would ask her to confess to a crime she never committed.

The clerk called August to the witness stand. He placed his right hand on the Bible and swore the oath, his composure flawless.

His lawyer stepped forward, guiding him with carefully crafted questions.

Avery (Counsel): "Mr. Pepper, how would you describe your marriage to Mrs. Sinclair during the early years?"

August: "Good. We built everything together— our home, our dreams, our faith. We prayed every night before bed. We served in ministry side by side. She was my best friend."

Vanessa's jaw tensed. Half-truths were always the most dangerous kind.

Avery: "And when did things begin to shift?"

August lowered his eyes, exhaling softly, as though the words themselves caused him pain. "At first, I wasn't so sure, but after reading an article on mental health, I realized she was burnt out from the regular routine of life… I should have been there more for her." Then he looked straight at her. "I'm really sorry, Vanessa."

She could see the sincerity in his eyes, feel it radiating from him—but that didn't soften the edge of betrayal she carried.

Avery: "So, you never addressed those changes with her?"

August: "I did, many times. I tried to be there more for her, I tried to shape myself into the man she wanted. I asked if she was okay, if we could talk. I believe she felt trapped, but it wasn't by me. It was by what was happening inside her, and I loved her. I still do. So I gave her space."

Avery: "So what led to the annulment?"

August: "She left. She said she couldn't breathe. That I was… not doing enough to be the man she wanted. That word hurt. It still hurts." His voice cracked just enough to sound human, to make the pain believable.

His lawyer placed a hand on the edge of the stand, lowering his tone. "Mr. Pepper, some might ask why you didn't challenge the annulment then."

"I didn't want to force her. I loved her too much for that. But time passed. I healed. And then this law came." He looked at the tribunal panel, calm and devout. "When I heard about the RBB Act, it felt like a door God opened. I thought… maybe this is His way of restoring what was broken."

A hush fell over the room. His words were smooth, practiced—but not manipulative. They sounded like a redemption arc.

The sharp-eyed board member leaned forward. "Mr. Pepper, do you believe your marriage can be reconciled now?"

"Yes," August said, with devastating certainty. "Because forgiveness is stronger than fear. Because I've prayed for her every night for five years. And because I know who she is beneath the pain. She's good, she's kind, and she's still my wife in the eyes of God."

Vanessa flinched at that last sentence, a small, involuntary movement. Her breath had caught, shallow and sudden. Ethan, sitting beside her, touched her knee lightly under the table, a quiet anchor in the storm.

Avery: "Would you be willing to undergo reconciliation measures?"

"Willing?" August repeated softly. "I want to. I've already done the work. I've changed. I've learned to lead with grace, not fear."

The lead reviewer folded his hands. "Thank you, Mr. Pepper. That was... heartfelt."

Of course it was. As August stepped down from the stand, he didn't meet her eyes, but Vanessa could feel the weight of his gaze lingering, a quiet pressure that seemed to press against her chest.

The clerk cleared his throat. "The respondent will now be called to testify."

Nadia leaned close, her whisper deliberate and calm. "Breathe. Don't give them what they expect. Tell the truth, not their version."

Vanessa nodded slightly and stood, each movement measured. Her palms were damp, slick against her coat. The usher extended the Bible. Vanessa hesitated for a heartbeat, fingers brushing the warm leather cover, familiar yet foreign in this room. Then she placed her hand on it and repeated the oath, her voice clear, steady despite the tremor in her stomach.

When she stepped up to the witness stand, the air seemed to shift around her. She wasn't August. She didn't carry a performance tucked behind her ribs, a carefully curated mask. She carried truth—and truth, in rooms like this, never came dressed in eloquence.

Nadia gave her a small, encouraging nod from the respondent's table. Vanessa returned it with a steadying breath, letting the moment settle before she spoke.

The lead reviewer leaned forward, tone neutral, professional. "Mrs. Sinclair," he began. "Please tell us why you believe your annulment should not be reconsidered under the Restore Broken Bridges Act."

Vanessa let the silence stretch. She didn't rush to fill it. Years of being spoken over had taught her the power of measured words, of claiming space that had been denied. This time, she would choose every word carefully.

"I left because I couldn't breathe," she said, voice quiet but firm, carrying more weight than it seemed.

The room remained still, the silence heavy, almost tangible. Somewhere in the gallery, a chair creaked, breaking the hush, but only slightly. The sound seemed to echo, a reminder that even small noises could punctuate truth in a space designed to scrutinize every word.

"I didn't leave because I fell out of love. I didn't leave because I wanted to chase something new. I left because being married to him felt like slowly erasing myself."

August sat motionless at his table. He tried to keep his face neutral, but Vanessa could see the tension in his jaw, the tight line betraying his calm.

She drew a small, steadying breath and continued. "He was kind. That's what makes it so hard to explain.

But he suffocated me. I was doing everything in the house. I was the provider. I was the support. I was the emotions… I was everything. And when I needed him to step up, he just suffocated me more. He tried, yes, but trying is not what I need. A marriage is not a place where you teach someone how to be there for you. I can't stay with someone who doesn't know how to catch me when I fall."

Vanessa's gaze settled on the sharp-faced woman on the board. "That's life in despair—being alone even in marriage, being too much because your partner doesn't know how to be enough… I don't want to go back to that."

Nadia's eyes flickered with pride and pain mingled together, a silent reassurance that Vanessa's words mattered.

The second board member cleared his throat, breaking the silence. "Mrs. Sinclair, what specific harm did you suffer? We need… clarity."

Of course they did. Harm, in their eyes, had to be visible—bruises, broken doors, shattered objects. Invisible bruises, the ones that steal your identity slowly, never counted enough.

Vanessa didn't flinch. "What harm is worse than disappearing without even realizing it?" she whispered, voice low but steady. "Every day, I lost a piece of myself until I couldn't even recognize my own voice."

The lead reviewer folded his hands. "Mrs. Sinclair, the petitioner has expressed deep regret. He claims he's changed. Does that not hold weight for you?"

Vanessa laughed softly, a dry, controlled sound. "Changed? Maybe he has. I hope he has. But this isn't about him anymore. This is about me, and I'm not obligated to walk back into a room that once burned me just because he says it's been cleaned."

The sharp-eyed woman shifted in her seat. Vanessa couldn't tell if it was discomfort or understanding. Maybe both.

Avery, August's lawyer, rose again. "Mrs. Sinclair, the Act is built on the principle of reconciliation— biblically encouraged reconciliation. Don't you believe in forgiveness?"

Vanessa's gaze fixed on him, steady and unwavering. "I forgave him a long time ago, but forgiveness isn't the same as returning."

A murmur rippled through the gallery. Someone on the panel whispered to a colleague, but Vanessa stayed focused, breathing deliberately, her words deliberate and unflinching.

"I don't hate him," she continued, her voice firm and controlled. "But forgiveness doesn't mean I owe him access to me again. It doesn't mean the law should drag me back here as if my freedom were a temporary privilege. What I built after leaving was not rebellion—it was survival. And no one has the right to take that away from me."

Avery tried again, softer this time. "Would you consider counseling as a step—"

"No," Vanessa said sharply, her tone final. It wasn't raised, it wasn't angry—it was unyielding. "I will not go to counseling to fix something I spent years trying to escape."

For the first time, August's carefully maintained mask flickered—a tiny crease between his brows, subtle but undeniable. Vanessa saw it and held her ground, letting the moment settle before she moved.

The sharp-faced reviewer leaned in slightly. "Mrs. Sinclair… you seem certain."

Vanessa met her gaze directly, unwavering. "Yes. I'm certain because I already spent years uncertain, and that nearly destroyed me."

The lead reviewer finally cleared his throat. "Thank you, Mrs. Sinclair. Your testimony has been noted."

As she stepped down from the stand, her knees were weak, but her spine remained straight. Each step toward Ethan and Nadia felt like emerging from deep water, lungs filling with air after being submerged.

Ethan rose slightly as she approached, his hand brushing reassuringly against her back. The simple touch grounded her, tethering her to someone who had seen her strength and her struggle.

"You did good," Nadia whispered, her voice low but warm. "You didn't just testify. You took the air back."

"Mrs. Sinclair," Avery's voice came, smooth and practiced now. "May I ask you a few follow-up questions?"

Vanessa nodded once. The tribunal's lead reviewer

gestured lightly. "You may proceed."

Avery stepped toward the stand with the measured calm of someone who had practiced this moment countless times in front of a mirror. He wasn't here to shout or intimidate. He didn't need to. Words were sharper when they masqueraded as kindness, a subtle blade wrapped in civility.

"You've spoken... powerfully," he began. "And I respect your courage. But we must return to the legal and spiritual purpose of this hearing. The Restore Broken Bridges Act is designed to assess whether a marriage was dissolved for biblical reasons. So, I'd like to clarify a few things. May I?"

"Go ahead," Vanessa said, steady but guarded, each word measured.

He stopped at just the right distance—close enough to apply pressure, far enough to maintain propriety. "You said you felt suffocated. But am I correct that there were no formal complaints filed during the marriage?"

Vanessa almost laughed, bitterly amused. Of course. There it was—the old metric. She answered evenly, almost mechanically. "No."

Avery's expression flickered briefly, a shadow crossing his practiced calm, but he recovered instantly. "Would you agree that many couples face difficulties in marriage? That some of the examples you gave, like suffocation, are not in themselves grounds for annulment, but rather signs of a need for reconciliation?"

A ripple of soft murmurs moved through the gallery again, like water brushing the sides of a boat. Avery raised a hand, as if calming those invisible waves. "I understand your perspective. But the law requires us to distinguish between actual legal cause and emotional interpretation."

Vanessa held her ground, her jaw set. Legal cause. Emotional interpretation. She had lived through both, and she knew which one had nearly destroyed her.

Her jaw clenched. "Emotional interpretation is still reality. Just because it didn't break a bone doesn't mean it didn't break something."

Avery nodded, a polite mask over an unreadable expression, like a man listening but not hearing.

"Understood. But—" He turned toward the panel now, shifting his tone deliberately. "—the petitioner has expressed repentance, has remained unmarried, and has shown clear intention to reconcile under biblical guidance. Would you not say this reflects the spirit of Matthew 5:23–24?"

The lead reviewer's eyes narrowed slightly in consideration. Vanessa could see where this was heading. They wanted to test her against Scripture, to turn faith into a measuring stick for her worthiness.

"I know that passage," Vanessa said calmly, voice steady but resonant. "Therefore, if you are offering your gift at the altar, remember that your brother has something against you, leave your gift there and first be reconciled to your brother." She met the reviewer's gaze directly, unwavering. "That passage isn't about forcing someone back into something that hurt them. It's about forgiveness. I forgave him years ago. But reconciliation is not an obligation."

Avery wasn't finished. "You remarried a few months ago, correct?"

"Yes."

"To Mr. Ethan Sinclair, who is seated beside you."

Vanessa felt Ethan's hand brush the inside of her wrist, a grounding touch amid the scrutiny. "Yes," she repeated, calm but firm.

"Would it be fair to say," Avery continued, voice deceptively neutral, "that your remarriage may influence your resistance to this review? That you have... something to protect?"

Vanessa blinked, letting the words land fully. "Of course I have something to protect," she said, voice sharp but controlled. "My family, my safety, my peace. I have everything to protect."

The room fell briefly silent, the gallery holding its breath as her words lingered. In that moment, Vanessa wasn't just a respondent. She was a woman claiming her boundaries, her life, and her dignity in a space designed to question both.

"But you understand," Avery pressed gently, "that the petitioner has a valid claim under this Act. That the law recognizes original covenantal priority."

Ethan stiffened beside her. He knew that phrase— he'd read the fine print of the law with her. *Original covenantal priority* meant the first marriage held spiritual precedence in tribunal review. It meant their marriage could be legally and religiously contested, even if it wasn't voided. It meant their home was no longer fully safe.

Vanessa swallowed hard, steadying herself. "I understand what the law says," she replied evenly. "But laws can be unjust."

Avery tilted his head slightly, as though pitying her. "Laws are written to protect sacred bonds."

She met his gaze, unwavering. "No. Sometimes laws are written to protect the people who hurt others in the name of God."

Her words landed like stones. A murmur broke through the gallery, spreading like wind through dry leaves. A bailiff's wooden staff banged sharply against the floor. "Order!"

The lead reviewer, Reverend Thomas Hale, adjusted his glasses and glanced down at his notes. To the panel's left, the wooden crucifix on the wall cast a long shadow across the floor, stretching toward Vanessa's chair. She felt its presence as keenly as any physical rope—a symbol of faith, twisted into law, reaching to bind her.

"Mrs. Sinclair," Hale said finally, his voice steady but carrying the weight of judgment, "before this panel withdraws to deliberate on the preliminary recommendation, you may make a final statement."

Vanessa inhaled slowly, letting the air fill her lungs and steel her nerves. Every eye in the room was on her. Every whispered judgment, every carefully hidden doubt, landed on her shoulders. And yet, for the first time in hours, she felt an unexpected lightness. She had the floor. She had the words. She had herself.

Vanessa rose slowly. Nadia gave the faintest nod from behind her stack of papers. *This is your moment*, it said without words. She faced the tribunal, three figures seated behind their polished wooden bench, with Avery and August to the side. August's face was unreadable now. Gone was the gentle, curated expression, replaced by something taut, restrained.

She cleared her throat. "At first, I married August Nathaniel Pepper because I believed in promises. I thought being a good wife meant becoming smaller. So

213

I folded myself up like a piece of paper. I learned to smile when I wanted to scream."

She let her words linger, letting the weight settle in the room. She wasn't trying to sound poetic. She was trying to be heard.

"Now the law says he has a right to call that erasure sacred," she continued, her voice steady. "The law says I owe him something because once upon a time, I said 'I do.' But I did not vow to lose myself. And I will not do it again."

Avery shifted slightly in his seat but didn't speak. This wasn't cross-examination anymore. This was truth delivered without apology.

Vanessa glanced briefly at August. His jaw was set, knuckles white against the table. For the first time since the hearing began, she didn't feel smaller beneath his gaze. She felt steady, grounded in herself.

"I've forgiven him," she said, her voice carrying through the chamber. "But forgiveness is not a bridge I have to cross with him on the other side. It's something I built inside myself so I could walk away."

Her words struck. Not everyone reacted, but

enough did. The sharp-faced woman on the panel, who had scrutinized every syllable, lowered her eyes. A subtle acknowledgment that some truths could not be ignored, no matter how uncomfortable.

Vanessa inhaled deeply, letting the air fill her chest. For the first time in hours, she felt fully present in this room—not a number, not a case, not someone else's definition of obedience. She was herself, entirely, and that alone felt like victory.

Vanessa took a step closer to the microphone. "I have a husband now. A home. And a child who finally laughs without flinching when someone knocks at the door. And if this Act was meant to mend what was broken, then maybe it should have started by protecting what's whole."

Her voice cracked, betraying the emotion she had held back for so long. "I will not go back—not legally, not emotionally, not spiritually. And if this law says my peace is negotiable, then this law is broken."

She stepped back from the mic slowly, letting the silence settle like a living thing in the room. It wasn't fragile anymore—it was heavy, undeniable, hers.

Ethan's chest swelled as he watched her, a quiet pride and relief washing over him. Nadia, ever vigilant, wiped the corner of one eye discreetly, a silent acknowledgment of the strength Vanessa had just displayed.

The lead reviewer cleared his throat, leaning toward his colleagues. They exchanged a few quiet words. Paper rustled. A pen tapped against polished wood. Then Hale straightened, voice formal but deliberate.

"This panel has heard all relevant testimonies and reviewed the circumstances," Hale began. "As required by Section 7, Subsection C of the Restore Broken Bridges Act, we will issue a preliminary recommendation before the final decision in thirty days. Our mandate," he continued, "is not to punish, but to preserve covenantal integrity. Yet we also recognize that reconciliation cannot be compelled by legal measures alone. We will therefore…" —he paused, letting the words hang— "…recommend that the original marriage remain under review, but that no compulsory mediation measure be enacted at this stage."

A subtle shift passed through the gallery. Relief, tension, acknowledgment—Vanessa felt it all. She had survived the scrutiny, claimed her truth, and for now, her life remained hers to hold. She looked to Ethan and saw the pride and steadfast support in his eyes, and for the first time in hours, she allowed herself to exhale fully.

Vanessa exhaled sharply. It wasn't a victory. But it wasn't a surrender either.

"This means," Nadia whispered from beside her, "they haven't forced reconciliation. They're leaving it open—but you're not being dragged into joint sessions. That's... something."

The panel rose. The bailiff called, "All rise." The tribunal exited in solemn order, their robes brushing softly against the polished wooden floor. The gallery began to empty, people filing out in murmurs, their footsteps echoing in the vast chamber.

Vanessa sank into her chair, finally allowing her body to sag with exhaustion. Ethan knelt slightly beside her, pressing his forehead gently to hers. His whisper was barely audible. "You were incredible."

She laughed—a soft, bitter, warm laugh that carried months of tension. "I almost threw up."

"Yeah," he said, brushing a hand across hers. "But you didn't."

Nadia slid into the seat next to her, stacking her files with the meticulous calm of a woman who had fought far harder battles. "They'll deliberate for weeks. August will likely push for a secondary review hearing. But today—you didn't give them a clean story to erase. You gave them yours."

Vanessa nodded slowly. The knot in her chest hadn't vanished, but it had loosened enough to let her breathe. Across the room, August stood with Avery, rigid and composed—but no longer smiling. The effort to appear gentle and contrite had faded, leaving only the weight of reality.

Outside the tribunal, the late-afternoon sun broke through thin clouds, casting pale gold across the steps. People passed her as she walked out—some indifferent, some curious, a few quietly respectful. The RBB Act might still have its claws in the edges of her life. But so did she, and her voice—once a quiet ache—now carried weight.

This isn't over, she thought, feeling the truth in her bones. *But neither am I.*

CHAPTER 17

The Quiet Work of Softening

Vanessa leaned forward, palms pressed flat against the cool porcelain sink, as a wave of nausea rolled through her. It wasn't sudden, and it wasn't the first time it had happened this week— or even today. But this one came slower, heavier, a pull that reached deep inside her. She closed her eyes and breathed through her mouth, willing her stomach to settle. She wasn't just fighting nausea; she was feeling it in every nerve, every cell. Her fingers curled slightly against the sink's smooth surface.

Her reflection in the mirror blurred, then steadied as she opened her eyes again. A slow breath escaped her lips, and the truth settled over her like a quiet tide.

She knew she was pregnant.

The word didn't frighten her the way it once would have. It didn't pierce her chest like an unexpected blow. Instead, it unfolded in her mind with a gentle inevitability. This time, she wasn't facing a storm alone. Her hand moved down toward her stomach. There was nothing to feel yet—no bump, no kicks, no fluttering—but the warmth of her palm pressed against her abdomen felt like a small promise.

Pregnancy had changed her once. It had taught her about fear, about how fragile hope could feel when it was tied to something so small, growing inside. But this time… this felt different. The difference wasn't in the symptoms; it was in her heart.

She turned the faucet, letting cold water run over her wrists, grounding herself in the sensation. Drops slid down her skin, clinging briefly before falling into the drain. The sound filled the quiet room like soft rain. She straightened slowly, lifting her chin just a little. Her face was pale, but her expression held something new—something steady.

Vanessa glanced at herself again. She didn't look

radiant or glowing. She didn't look like someone in a picture-perfect announcement photo. She looked real, and for the first time, that was enough. Reaching for a paper towel, she dabbed at her face, then whispered to her reflection almost without thinking.

"It's okay. We're okay."

When Vanessa stepped out of the bathroom, the hallway felt too bright at first. The clinic's fluorescent lights flattened everything—faces, colors, even moments that were supposed to feel significant. Ethan sat near the end of the corridor, just where she knew he'd be. His elbows rested on his knees, hands loosely clasped, head tilted slightly down. He wasn't pacing, wasn't checking his watch, wasn't asking questions. He was simply there.

For a moment, she just watched him. Watched the rise and fall of his shoulders, the soft tap of his foot against the floor—not impatiently, just enough to show he hadn't drifted away. She had known him long enough to recognize this version of him. This was the Ethan who always showed up.

She exhaled slowly, and the sound made him look

up. His eyes found hers, and a warmth flickered across his face. He straightened slightly, but didn't rush toward her. Ethan never did. He waited for her to decide what the moment needed.

Vanessa walked toward him, her hands still slightly damp from the sink. The nausea had receded into the background, leaving a dull hum that matched the quiet beat of her heart. She stopped a few feet away. The space between them carried its own unspoken weight.

"You okay?" he asked softly.

The question wasn't loaded. It didn't demand an answer. It was simply a place for her to land, if she wanted. She nodded. She was okay. She was standing, breathing, holding something fragile inside her with a steadier heart than before.

Ethan took a step to close the gap completely. Vanessa didn't hesitate. She reached out, and he met her halfway. His hand wrapped around hers gently, as if holding a piece of glass that mattered. The hallway around them blurred into a soft hum of distant voices and the faint beeping of a machine down the corridor.

"I don't want you to feel like you have to say

anything," she murmured.

He squeezed her hand once. "I know."

The simplicity of that answer steadied her more than any words could have. She had expected—maybe even prepared for—a speech about how everything would be fine, a reassurance delivered in big, sweeping statements. But Ethan had never been a man of unnecessary promises. When life got heavy, when the world pressed down too hard, he didn't try to fix her. He didn't overcomplicate. He simply stayed. That presence alone was enough.

Vanessa leaned her shoulder lightly against the wall, their joined hands resting between them. The coolness of the paint pressed against her skin grounded her, and she let herself draw a slow, steadying breath.

"This time feels different," she admitted, her voice barely above the quiet hum of the corridor.

Ethan didn't ask her to explain. He didn't press. He just nodded, the corners of his mouth lifting ever so slightly. "Yeah," he said quietly. "It does."

His thumb brushed against the back of her hand in a small, steady motion. Each movement was deliberate, unhurried, carrying more weight than any grand declaration. Vanessa drew in a shaky breath, holding it for a heartbeat before letting it escape slowly. She wasn't floating, wasn't radiant, wasn't swept up in some fairytale rush. She was simply here. Standing. Breathing. Safe. And for now, that was more than enough.

Ethan reached out with his other hand and tucked a loose strand of hair behind her ear. The touch was gentle, tender, but not cloying. He leaned his forehead against hers for the briefest second, and in that quiet press, Vanessa felt something anchor itself firmly in her chest. A slow, steady pulse of reassurance, of presence, of something unshakable.

She didn't need grand gestures. She didn't need words that promised forever. She needed this. Him. The weight of his presence and the quiet certainty of his care. And for the first time since stepping into that clinic, she allowed herself to imagine that maybe, just maybe, this could be different.

Her heart thudded against her ribs in a new rhythm—not frantic, not tentative, but steady. A rhythm that matched his hand in hers, his forehead to hers, the subtle promise that whatever came next, she wouldn't have to face it alone.

The days that followed unfolded without fanfare. There were no big announcements, no neatly framed ultrasound photos on the fridge. No glittering celebrations, only quiet shifts: the small ways life softened around them. She noticed how Ethan stopped flipping on the harsh overhead light first thing in the morning. Instead, he cracked the curtain just enough to let a strip of early sunlight stretch across the room. The light felt gentler that way, bathing everything in a quiet warmth, like the world itself had slowed just enough to let them breathe.

Vanessa moved slower too. There was no race to prove she was strong or brave. This time, she allowed tenderness in. She let the morning nausea come and go without resentment. She rested her palm on her belly without whispering prayers soaked in fear. It was strange, this kind of peace—soft, steady, unassuming.

They didn't talk endlessly about the pregnancy. Ethan didn't flood her with baby name lists or plans for a nursery. Instead, he lingered in moments that demanded nothing from them. Sitting with her on the porch steps in the evening, listening when she spoke, even when the words came unpolished or fragmented. Simply being there.

One quiet afternoon, Vanessa sat cross-legged on the floor, folding tiny clothes. She wasn't even sure why she had taken them out so early—there was no nursery yet, no shelf waiting. Just a small cardboard box of hand-me-downs a friend had sent. She ran her fingers over the soft cotton, pausing on a little cream-colored onesie with a faint sun stitched over the heart. She traced the tiny embroidery with her thumb, and the weight of the moment settled over her, both heavy and light at once.

Ethan walked in quietly, carrying two mugs of tea. He didn't ask what she was doing. He simply set the mugs down, lowered himself beside her, and reached into the box. His fingers brushed over the folded clothes carefully, as though touching something precious. Vanessa watched him in silence, her heart swelling at the gentleness in his movements.

He lifted one of the tiny socks between thumb and forefinger, squinting at how impossibly small it was. A soft laugh escaped him, half in wonder, half in disbelief. The sound was a quiet thread weaving through the room, binding the moment, binding them.

"They're so little," he said quietly.

She smiled, tracing the edge of the onesie with her thumb. "Yeah."

For a long moment, neither of them spoke. The silence between them was tender, warm, a presence more comforting than any words. Vanessa leaned back slightly, hands resting over her stomach. She wasn't showing much yet, but she could feel it. Her body knew, and slowly, she was allowing herself to trust that knowledge.

Ethan leaned his shoulder against hers, and their shared stillness spoke in a language all its own. No grand speeches. No promises written in the air. Just presence.

"I don't want this to be something we survive," she said finally, her voice soft, careful. "I want it to be something we live through. Together."

Ethan's hand found hers, warm and grounding. "Then we'll live it," he answered simply.

His words weren't a declaration—they were a choice. A quiet, everyday choice, made in the space between them. Vanessa exhaled slowly, letting the weight of his presence fill the room around her.

The kind of light they carried wasn't loud or dramatic. It didn't erase the fears, the lingering echoes of loss, or the memories of what had come before. But it glowed. A steady, quiet warmth that seeped into the spaces they had once left empty.

As she rested her head lightly against Ethan's shoulder, Vanessa felt the shift—small, almost imperceptible, but real. A future was forming, because this time they were preparing for it. Not with cribs or checklists alone, but with the quiet work of softening, of being present, of holding each other through the everyday moments that mattered most.

CHAPTER 18

When Grace Demands Courage

The lecture hall smelled faintly of chalk and old wood, a scent Ethan had long associated with certainty. Standing at the front of the room, where he had spent years lecturing on ethical markets and financial integrity, he adjusted his notes without really seeing them. The board behind him remained half-covered with yesterday's formulas, a ghost of lessons past. Normally, this space calmed him. Today, it felt more like standing on cracked ice.

He had built his reputation on two foundations: legal integrity and scriptural principle. For him, they were not opposing forces but twin anchors. The law gave structure; scripture gave soul. Grace wove quietly between them, a subtle thread that gave room to breathe. He had always told his students that every ethical dilemma was not a war but a crossroads where principle met conscience.

Yet principles were easy to preach when they weren't burning through your own home. Outside, the RBB Act had grown louder. The policy, dressed in the language of "restoration," was forcing people like Vanessa back into the scrutiny of their pasts. She hadn't asked for this fight. Neither had he. But here it was, relentless and unavoidable.

That afternoon, he returned home and saw her sitting at the dinner table. Ethan didn't need her to speak to read the tension etched across her face. Her expression was tight around the edges, the faint traces of sleeplessness and worry lingering there, but her eyes betrayed her: wet, heavy with the weight of what was coming.

"They want us to testify again," she said quietly, placing a folded envelope on his desk.

He blinked, trying to process it. "When?"

"Next month. Publicly."

The words hung between them, heavier than any formula he had ever written on the board. Ethan felt the room close in around him, the lecture hall's structure, the weight of law and conscience, all seeming to shrink into this single, unyielding moment.

The word hung in the air like smoke. *Publicly.*

It meant the press. It meant the university board watching. It meant the church-affiliated trustees, who already labeled him a "moderate voice" with wary politeness. It meant choosing sides in a battle where neutrality would be its own kind of betrayal.

Ethan sank slowly into his chair, the envelope resting between them like a live wire. It seemed to hum with everything unspoken—the risk, the exposure, the cost. He had spent years building a career that balanced on principle and patience. He had fought for the kind of classroom where faith and conscience could share the same air without suffocating each other. Now, that same voice—the one he had spent a lifetime cultivating—might cost him everything.

Vanessa shifted her weight, crossing her arms against her chest as if to hold herself together. "I need to know where you stand," she whispered. "Not as a professor or as a theologian. *You.*"

Ethan opened his mouth, but the words tangled in his throat. He believed in grace. He believed in conscience. He believed that truth and mercy could coexist. But belief alone wasn't enough to shield them from the board's politics or the church's judgment. The trustees—the same men who shook his hand on Sundays and quoted him in articles—didn't care about grace. They cared about control.

Silence filled the space between them, sharp and heavy. Vanessa's gaze held his, steady but trembling at the edges. Something in her posture shifted—a flicker of hurt, a shadow of memory crossing her face.

"Ethan," she said softly, "I'm not asking you to fix this. I just need to know if you're with me in it."

The honesty in her voice stripped away every place he could hide. He looked down at his hands—the same hands that had written lectures about integrity, the same hands that once signed his name on petitions for reform, the same hands that now trembled slightly against the desk. Hands that could shape arguments

233

and influence policy, but what good were they if he couldn't hold on to what mattered most?

And still, fear whispered.

Fear of losing the job that had become his identity.

Fear of watching his years of careful work unravel overnight.

Fear of being labeled *dangerous*.

Vanessa's voice cracked as she whispered, "Please don't stay silent."

The words pierced through the air like a prayer and a plea at once.

Ethan lifted his eyes to hers, and for a heartbeat, he saw everything she wasn't saying—the exhaustion, the faith, the history that had taught her silence was its own kind of wound.

He drew a slow breath, the sound rough in his throat, and for the first time since the envelope landed on the table, he felt the full gravity of the choice waiting for him.

But Ethan, for the first time in years, didn't have an answer ready.

Vanessa didn't sleep that night. The house was too

quiet. She lay in bed staring at the ceiling, fingers splayed over her stomach as if anchoring herself to the present. Yet the past kept crawling in, insistent and uninvited. She thought of the years she'd spent piecing her life back together, of the way happiness had seeped in like light through a cracked door. And now—this. Another courtroom. Another fight for legitimacy.

She whispered into the darkness, "Why is my healing considered a sin by others?"

The question wasn't meant for Ethan. It wasn't even meant for God. It was the raw ache of someone who had spent too long defending her right to be happy.

Ethan was in the next room, the soft glow of his study light spilling into the hallway. She could hear the occasional turn of paper, the creak of his chair. He was thinking—measuring, weighing, balancing. It would have been easier if he were cruel. If he had simply chosen a side against her. But this hesitation—this quiet, careful pause—cut deeper. Because it meant he cared. And caring made betrayal sharper.

By dawn, she sat at the kitchen table wrapped in a

sweater, watching the sun inch slowly across the floorboards. The kettle whistled, a lone sharp sound in the early light. Ethan entered the kitchen, looking as though the night had passed over him like a storm. His tie hung loose, his shirt wrinkled, the lines of exhaustion etched into his face.

"You didn't sleep either," she said softly, her voice almost swallowed by the morning.

He poured himself tea without answering, the steam rising in thin, curling tendrils between them. Then, slowly, he sat down across from her, eyes heavy, expression taut with the weight of the choice he still hadn't voiced.

"Vanessa," he began, voice low, careful. "You know what the board is like. If I speak out against the Act, I'll lose my position. It won't just be my lectures they silence. It'll be everything I've worked for."

She stared at the steam curling from her cup. "I'm not asking you to throw away your life."

"But you are asking me to take a stand," he said, almost gently.

She met his eyes, steady and unflinching. "I'm

asking you not to leave me standing alone."

The weight of those words pressed into the room like a living thing. Ethan swallowed. He wanted to protect everything he had built—the lectures, the influence, the platform he had spent years carving out—but for the first time, he realized that protecting it might mean losing her.

"I want to fight," he said, voice strained. "But if I lose my voice, if I lose my platform—"

"Then maybe," she interrupted softly, "your platform isn't what's giving you your voice."

The silence that followed was unbearable and sacred all at once. He could feel the gravity of the choice pressing down, the stark reality of what loyalty and courage demanded. Protecting his career no longer felt like the right measure of integrity. His priorities had shifted. By the time the first light of morning brushed the kitchen floor, Ethan had made his decision. Vanessa mattered more than anything else. If standing by her meant risking everything else, then he was ready. He would do right by her.

The summons had arrived. Their names were on

the list to testify before the public hearing. Ethan stood beside Vanessa at the courthouse steps, the air heavy with anticipation. A protest had formed across the street. Some held signs defending the Act, their voices loud, insistent. Others challenged it, shouting, waving placards, demanding attention. A reporter's camera swept across the crowd, catching every movement, every expression. Vanessa's pulse thudded in her ears, echoing the rhythm of the city's tension around them.

Ethan's hand found hers. She squeezed it, and for a fleeting moment, the chaos faded into the weight of their joined presence. Whatever came next, they would face it together.

She whispered, "If this is too much, I'll walk away. You don't have to choose me over everything you've built."

His eyes flicked toward her, sharp, unwavering. "Vanessa, don't you dare make yourself smaller for their comfort."

She blinked at him, and something in his voice made her heart trip. He hadn't chosen yet. Not fully. But she could feel the battle inside him burning—each pulse of it echoing the courage they would need together.

They entered the packed chamber. Rows of officials, church leaders, reporters, and onlookers pressed against every available seat. A cross hung at the front of the room, next to the seal of the reviewing board. The symbolism was not subtle, and Vanessa felt her heartbeat echo in her palms as she took her place at the witness table.

Ethan sat beside her, hands folded tightly in his lap. He could feel the weight of a hundred eyes on him— the professor, the man with influence, the one people thought they knew. Each gaze seemed to measure, judge, and catalog him.

The chairman cleared his throat. "Professor Collins," he began, "your institution stands in full support of the RBB Act. Do you stand with them?"

Ethan inhaled slowly. He could take the easy path. He could nod politely, wrap his answer in careful academic neutrality, and go home to continue teaching about integrity from the safety of quiet compromise. But then he looked at Vanessa. At the woman who had walked through fire just to live again. At the way she carried herself now—not with pride, not with defiance, but with steady, undeniable dignity.

And suddenly, neutrality tasted like ash.

He rose slowly. The microphone caught the tremor in his breath, amplifying the human weight beneath his words. "I've spent my career teaching students that integrity isn't real unless it costs something," he began, his voice low but clear. "I've taught that the law should protect the vulnerable, not trap them. And I've taught that faith without grace is nothing but control dressed up as virtue."

A murmur rippled through the room—shifting bodies, rustling papers, the uneasy whisper of those who weren't sure whether to applaud or recoil. Ethan steadied his voice, one hand braced lightly against the table as though to ground himself. "I cannot stand behind a law that punishes someone for healing. I will not endorse shame disguised as righteousness."

He glanced at Vanessa then, his eyes steady, his voice firm. "I choose to stand with her."

The silence that followed was the kind that

demanded reverence. A single cough broke it, then the sound of camera shutters—a staccato rhythm marking the moment his life changed.

The chairman leaned forward, his expression pinched. "Professor Collins, you understand what this means for your employment?"

Ethan nodded once, calm. "Yes," he said quietly. "I do."

And in that stillness, something in him broke free. The fear that had haunted him for weeks cracked open, replaced by a strange, steady peace.

When they finally stepped out of the chamber, the air hit them like a new season—cooler, cleaner, alive with the hum of a crowd that didn't know whether to cheer or condemn. Reporters swarmed the steps, microphones flashing. Ethan's phone vibrated endlessly in his pocket—messages flooding in, some full of outrage, others of quiet gratitude. But he didn't look.

Vanessa stood beside him, wind lifting strands of her hair. The sunlight spilled across the courthouse steps like a benediction. She turned toward him, her voice almost a whisper. "You just threw away your job."

He looked at her, a faint smile ghosting across his lips. "No," he said. "I just stopped letting it own me."

For a moment, she couldn't speak. Tears blurred her vision, soft and hot, and she reached for his hand. He met her halfway, his grip steady and sure, grounding her in that impossible mix of grief and hope.

She thought of every version of herself that had stood in front of a judge, every time she'd had to justify her existence. And now—here she was. Not alone. Not silenced.

She squeezed his hand tighter. "You didn't have to do this," she whispered.

"I know," he said. "That's why it mattered."

And as the cameras flashed and the world kept turning, Vanessa realized she wasn't just grateful he'd stood beside her—she was grateful she'd chosen a man who understood that love, at its truest, was an act of courage.

Two days later, Vanessa met August. The man who had once been her husband sat across from her in a small, windowless room, the smell of stale coffee clinging to the air like a stubborn memory. His hands were folded loosely on the table, his posture careful, guarded. He didn't deny it. He had triggered the review, whether out of resentment, a sense of obligation, or a shadow of guilt—it didn't matter.

"I didn't know they'd take it this far," he muttered, eyes flicking toward hers.

Vanessa studied him. August was a man who had built walls and called them penance. She could feel anger simmering in the back of her throat, hot and familiar, the old ache of past betrayals. But then something else rose up, slower and quieter.

She exhaled, letting the air carry the weight of years spent surviving. "I forgive you."

The words didn't excuse him. They didn't erase the hurt or the ways he had failed her. But they freed her. A quiet relief unfurled inside her chest, spreading warmth through the tension that had followed her like a shadow.

She rose from the table, shoulders squared but heart lighter, and walked out into the bright afternoon. Ethan waited outside, leaning casually against the car, but his eyes were all focus—steady, sure, unwavering.

The future wasn't clean. It wasn't easy. There would be challenges, days of exhaustion, moments of fear. But it was theirs.

As Ethan slipped his hand into hers, Vanessa felt the light she had carried for months grow steadier, stronger, anchored in something enduring. She glanced at him, and he offered the faintest smile, one that carried everything: solidarity, love, courage. Together, they stepped forward, ready to meet whatever came next.

CHAPTER 19

The Sound of a Beginning

The air in the ultrasound room felt softer than most hospital spaces. Overhead lights were dimmed, the monitor angled toward the bed, and the faint hum of jazz drifted from a hidden speaker near the ceiling. Someone had thought about the details—how light and sound could soften a moment, make it feel almost sacred.

Vanessa lay back on the padded table, the paper beneath her crinkling as she shifted. The gel bottle sat on the counter, uncapped and waiting. The technician, a woman with kind eyes and a calm smile, adjusted her gloves while humming along with the music.

Ethan stood beside Vanessa, his hand enveloping

hers. Their fingers intertwined, settled into a quiet rhythm they had learned together over time. Vanessa's pulse was steady—not from lack of emotion, but from the kind of steadiness that only comes after walking through storms.

The technician rolled the cart closer. "All right," she said softly. "Ready to meet your little one?"

Vanessa nodded. Ethan exhaled, a sound neither nervous nor casual—it was reverent, as if honoring the moment they had waited for so long.

Cool gel spread across Vanessa's lower belly. The wand pressed gently, and the image flickered to life on the black screen above them. At first, it was just a blur of gray and light. Then a heartbeat filled the room—a rapid, fluttering rhythm like wings beating too fast to stop, yet determined. Vanessa blinked, and a tear slipped free before she could catch it. She had prepared herself for this, rehearsed it in her mind a hundred times. But nothing, nothing could have prepared her for this.

The technician angled the probe carefully. "There we go..." she murmured. "And... that's your baby."

Ethan leaned forward instinctively, his hand tightening around Vanessa's. His breath caught, not from the image itself, but from everything wrapped around it—months of questions, of choosing love over silence, of standing in rooms where they had both felt too small. And now this heartbeat, fierce and bright, filled the room like a quiet miracle.

Vanessa turned her head toward him. He was staring at the screen as if it were the first star he had ever seen.

"Ethan," she whispered.

He glanced down at her, eyes already glistening. "We're bringing light into the world," he said softly. "Not just a child."

The technician smiled knowingly but said nothing. She had seen enough families to recognize a sacred moment when it happened. Later, when the image was printed and placed carefully in a slim envelope, Vanessa sat on the edge of the exam table, legs dangling just a little, holding the tiny printout as if it were already a part of her heart.

"I used to think joy had to be earned," Vanessa said

quietly, still staring at the picture. "Like it was something you got only after proving you'd suffered enough."

Ethan moved closer, close enough that she could feel the warmth radiating from him. "But it doesn't," he said softly.

"No," she whispered, her voice catching just a little. "It doesn't."

He reached for her hand again, their fingers tangling naturally, a silent language they had learned without ever speaking it. The moment didn't erase the hard things. It didn't rewrite the past. It simply reminded them that light could bloom in the middle of ruins. Vanessa closed her eyes for a moment, letting that quiet truth settle deep inside her.

"I think she already knows she's loved," Ethan murmured, voice gentle, full of wonder.

Vanessa smiled through quiet tears. "Yeah. I think so too."

They left the clinic hand in hand, stepping out into an afternoon washed with soft, golden light. The air was cool, scented faintly with rain that hadn't yet decided to fall. Cars passed slowly on the street, and somewhere nearby, laughter broke the hum of ordinary life. Life kept moving, but for them, the world felt suspended, held in a fragile, perfect pause.

Ethan carried the envelope carefully in his other hand, the way someone might hold a treasure too precious to risk. He wasn't thinking about the job he had lost, the endless board meetings, or the whispers that still swirled around their names. For once, he was just here—with her, and with the tiny heartbeat that had changed everything.

Vanessa walked a little slower than usual, feeling as if each step pressed a small promise into the pavement beneath them. She had spent too many years rushing forward, bracing for impact. But this moment—this simple, quiet walk with him—felt like being allowed to arrive, to finally breathe.

They stopped at the corner by the park. Leaves drifted lazily from the trees, catching the sunlight like fragments of gold. Ethan tucked the envelope into his jacket pocket, keeping it close to his heart, a silent vow of all they had endured and all they would cherish. For a heartbeat, everything else faded. It was just them, the day, and the tiny life that had already brought them more light than they had dared to imagine.

Vanessa turned to him. "Do you ever think about how much we've lost?" she asked softly.

Ethan hesitated. "All the time."

"And yet," she continued, "we're still here."

He nodded. "And she's here too."

They stood like that for a long moment, words unnecessary. She leaned into him, and he wrapped his arm around her shoulders, his hand resting protectively near the space where their daughter was growing.

"I used to be afraid of being seen," Vanessa admitted quietly. "Afraid of being judged—for choosing to live again. For choosing you. For choosing me."

Ethan pressed a gentle kiss to the top of her head. "They can judge all they want. But they don't get to write our story."

She tilted her head toward him, eyes shimmering in the soft afternoon light. "No. They don't."

The sun dipped lower, bathing the park in a glow

that softened every edge, every shadow. It wasn't a grand ending or a loud declaration—just a quiet beginning. Ethan reached into his pocket and drew out the photo again. Vanessa placed her hand over his, their fingers pressing lightly, tenderly. Together, they stared at it, two souls letting joy settle fully in the space where fear had once ruled.

"She's going to know she was wanted," Vanessa whispered.

Ethan nodded, voice steady and warm. "She already does."

Vanessa exhaled softly, leaning against him as the world moved quietly around them. The past no longer defined her. The future wasn't something to fear. And the heartbeat that had fluttered inside that dimly lit exam room was more than just a sound—it was a beginning, a pulse that promised love, resilience, and all the light they had waited so long to find.

CHAPTER 20

Lila Grace

The hospital room smelled faintly of antiseptic and lavender, a combination that felt both sterile and strangely comforting. The lights were low, muted to a soft amber glow. Outside the door, nurses moved in quiet patterns, their voices hushed, shoes whispering against the polished floor. Somewhere down the hall, a baby cried — a thin, bright sound that cut through the night like a small, distant star.

Vanessa gripped Ethan's hand with every ounce of strength she had left. Damp strands of hair clung to her forehead, and each breath came in heavy, uneven pulls. Hours had passed. Maybe it had been a whole night. Maybe longer. Time had begun to fold in on itself after the fifth contraction.

Ethan had not let go once. His thumb traced slow, steady circles over her knuckles. Between her breaths, he whispered words that weren't from any childbirth book — just raw, urgent, and intimate:

"I'm here."

"You've got this."

"Look at me."

Vanessa focused on his voice as the room tilted and pulsed around her. Contractions came like a tide she could not command — crashing, retreating, then rising again, each wave higher, stronger, and more relentless. She squeezed her eyes shut and imagined the nursery at home: soft forest-green walls, a mobile spinning lazily above the crib, the tiny white onesie folded neatly on the dresser. She had spent countless nights in that room, dreaming of this moment. But her imagination had always been a quiet echo compared to the fierce, primal reality now claiming her body.

The doctor stood at the foot of the bed. "You're doing beautifully," she said, her voice both gentle and unwavering. "One more push, Vanessa. Just one more."

Vanessa nodded weakly, then found a steadier strength in the motion. She felt Ethan's forehead press against hers, his breath mingling with her own, steadying her in ways words could not. His hand tightened around hers, warm and unyielding.

"You're stronger than this," he whispered.

And for the first time that night, Vanessa believed him. She gathered what felt like the last reserves of her strength, drawing not only from her body but from every piece of herself that had survived the years of struggle. The courtroom battles. The whispered judgments behind closed doors. The heartache she had carried like a shadow. The choice to love again despite the fear of loss. The choice to keep going even when it had seemed impossible.

Her body coiled with determination. The room grew still, as if the world itself was pausing in anticipation. Then came a cry.

A small, fierce, beautiful sound that broke through the heavy air. At first it was fragile, fluttering like a note at the beginning of a song, barely there, uncertain. But it grew, strong and insistent, filling the room with life, scattering the shadows, reaching even the corners that had held worry and fear.

Vanessa's chest shook with a sob she had not expected. She tried to speak, to cry, but all she could do was feel the tremor of wonder coursing through her. The doctor lifted a tiny, wrinkled baby, soft as morning light, a gentle shade of pink, slick with newness and miracle. The nurse moved with calm precision, supporting the fragile form.

"You have a daughter," the doctor said, her voice warm, quiet with triumph.

Ethan's knees nearly gave out. He reached for Vanessa, for the baby, for everything that had led them to this moment. The nurse placed the small bundle against Vanessa's chest. Her arms curved instinctively, as though they had been waiting all her life to hold this new life, to cradle this perfect weight.

The baby's tiny fingers curled around Vanessa's, grasping with a strength that belied her size. Her breath was uneven and sweet, a tiny rhythm that anchored

Vanessa in the room, in the moment, in the overwhelming miracle of now. Ethan bent close, tears pooling in his eyes, whispering words that were too full to leave his lips but too necessary to keep inside.

Vanessa pressed her cheek to the baby's soft head, feeling warmth, life, and the culmination of every choice that had brought her here. The hospital room, with its antiseptic and lavender scent, seemed to glow, a quiet sanctuary holding the first fragile moments of a new family.

The world outside that room blurred and fell away. Nothing existed beyond this small, glowing space. All that remained was this: a heartbeat pressing against her heartbeat. A breath meeting a breath. Ethan leaned closer, resting his forehead against Vanessa's temple. He inhaled the faint warmth of her skin, the sharp cleanliness of antiseptic, and the delicate sweetness of newborn air.

"She's perfect," he whispered, his voice low and full of awe.

Vanessa laughed, but it broke into a choked, trembling sound. "She's real," she whispered back, tears tracing quiet paths down her cheeks.

The baby blinked at them, her tiny eyelids fluttering like fragile wings. She let out another soft cry, smaller than before, and her fingers opened and closed against Vanessa's skin, seeking warmth and someone to call home.

The nurse moved quietly among the monitors, checking numbers and charts without breaking the spell of the moment. Then she looked up at them, her voice gentle. "What do we call her?"

Vanessa met Ethan's gaze, and for a heartbeat, no words were needed. Everything they had felt, feared, and hoped for was held in that look.

"Lila," Vanessa whispered, her voice soft but certain.

"Lila Grace," Ethan added, his lips brushing her hair as he spoke.

The nurse's smile deepened, full of quiet joy and pride. "Welcome to the world, Lila Grace," she said, her words wrapping the room in warmth.

Vanessa traced the curve of Lila's cheek with a finger, marveling at the softness and the perfect weight of her. She thought of Miles, imagining his wide-eyed excitement when he finally met his new little sister. Every heartbeat, every breath in this room, felt like the start of something unbreakable, a family stitched together with love, hope, and everything they had endured to arrive here.

Lila's cry had softened to a quiet hum, as if she already knew she was safe and home. Outside the window, the first light of dawn crept slowly across the sky, spilling gold over the city and turning the glass to molten warmth. The room had quieted completely. Nurses moved with gentle precision, dimming the lights further, while the machines hummed a soft, steady rhythm in the background.

Ethan sat at the edge of the bed, one hand resting lightly on Vanessa's shoulder, the other cradling the small bundle in her arms. Lila lay against Vanessa's chest, wrapped in a pale cotton blanket. Her breathing was even and light, a gentle, rhythmic whisper that made the whole world seem slower, softer, and impossibly still. Vanessa brushed a fingertip over the downy hair on Lila's head. She had always imagined this moment as a celebration — a flurry of people, cameras flashing, voices rising in excitement. But this quiet, this perfect stillness, was far better.

Ethan tilted his head, watching the two of them. He had always thought he understood love, but this— this was something older, deeper, and beyond the reach of words.

"I didn't know it would feel like this," he murmured.

Vanessa looked up at him, exhausted but radiant, her cheeks flushed, her eyes shining with quiet wonder. "Like what?"

"Like… the world just shifted," he said, his voice low, almost reverent.

She smiled faintly, letting the corners of her mouth lift. "It did," she whispered.

Vanessa laughed softly, a fragile, happy sound that wrapped around them both like a warm blanket. She looked at him — not the professor with principles, not the man who had stood in courtrooms to defend what was right, but Ethan: the man who had stood beside her through every contraction, every ache, every storm.

The man who had been steady when the world was anything but.

"I love you," she said quietly.

Ethan's breath caught. He pressed a kiss to her forehead, then to Lila's tiny hand, marveling at how something so small could hold so much of his heart. "I love you both," he whispered, his voice thick with wonder.

Outside, the sun climbed higher, painting the sky in slow bands of gold. The city below began to stir — cars moving along wet streets, footsteps echoing against sidewalks, the hum of ordinary life waking to a new day. But inside this small room, time seemed to pause, as if the world itself understood that something sacred had just begun.

Vanessa leaned back against the pillows, her body drained but her heart wide open. Ethan stayed beside her, his hand resting over both hers and Lila's, anchoring them together in quiet, steady warmth.

For the first time in a long time, the word *arrival* did not mean the end of something hard fought or painfully lost. It meant the beginning — of a new rhythm, a new peace, and a love that had found its way through every shadow to reach the light.

Afterword

When I sat with this chapter of Vanessa's life, one question wouldn't leave me: what do we call love after the papers say "enough"? This book gave me a clear answer, sometimes we call it honesty. Here, love sheds its costumes, paper walls collapse, courthouse benches, and kitchen ledgers keep score. Survival shows up first, loyal as a stray dog. But survival is a floor, not a home. Peace arrives where respect lives, where attention is paid, where apology is followed by practice.

She comes to realize silence is not safety, habit is not devotion, and that a child's steadiness matters more than grownups' pride. She finds a faith that hums from the back row. She accepts gifts with open eyes, coffee, a book, a steady presence, and returns the ones tied with carelessness. For her, boundaries become her grammar, dignity her voice, patience the scaffolding, and accountability the nails that hold it all together. She builds the room with consistency.

Of these, if one line lingers, let it be this: love is not the heat of one night or the ceremony of one morning; it is the daily craft of regard. It doesn't reduce people to bodies or promises to paperwork. It chooses truth in small rooms, at the sink, at the door, before a sleeping child, and chooses again tomorrow.

Thanks for walking her through debt notices and soft beginnings, court dates, and cinnamon-roll Sundays. May you leave believing that endings can be mercies, beginnings quiet, and that choosing yourself is not abandonment, but rather alignment.

Until the next story, may you keep a tender ledger: pay attention, spend grace, and balance life in love.

Vanessa walked away to have a future.

Now the law—and her past—want her back.

Renewing their vows was supposed to save Vanessa and August's marriage. Instead, it broke it for good. Now, with the papers signed, Vanessa is learning what freedom feels like for her and her son… and how lonely it can be.

Then Ethan shows up. Calm where August was controlling. Steady when her life was pure chaos. He doesn't ask her to shrink, only to breathe. And for the first time in years, she does.

But just as Vanessa starts to believe in love again, the past finds a way to rewrite itself. A new law puts her divorce in jeopardy—and threatens the life she's building.

Caught between who she was and who she's becoming, Vanessa must decide what it really means to fight for freedom, for love, and for her future.

August wants her back.

She wants freedom and a future.

Ethan just wants her … to be happy.